THE
JACKASS ALLIANCE

ROBERT ESPENSCHEID JR.

ISBN: 1466204257

ISBN 13: 9781466204256

Library of Congress Control Number: 2011914047

CreateSpace, North Charleston, SC

CREDITS

Bob Dylan (paraphrased song lyrics):

> Sweetheart Like You
>
> Slow Train
>
> It's Alright, Ma (I'm Only Bleeding)

SETTING THE STAGE

TROOP 822

Maddy: "Our cause is just!"

Ana: "So was Davito Crockett's, and a lot of good it did him."

To Andy
maximum shovelhead gearhead

and to
the Scouts at Little Sioux, June 2008

ACKNOWLEDGMENTS

First and foremost to Jodilyn Stuart, Holly Hendren, writer pal Sherri Cropper, Janell Meador, and Hop Wechsler for editing/critiquing through the early efforts. The thumbs-up encouragement was heaven sent.

A special thanks to Mark E. Easter, D.O., and Amanda Lewis at KCCI TV for their time, knowledge, and enthusiasm.

Much appreciation to Rob Rolfe, Dr. Joel Baker, Jack Gittinger, Brad Olk at WHO TV, Keith Hinds, Shannon Colyer, Greg Cummings, Denise Elefson, Kristin Salmi, Leah McIntire, Pete Robertson, and the Southern Iowa Oak Savannah Alliance.

To the impressionists: Cecile Broz (artbycecile.com) for allowing the appropriation of her print, *Dry Dog Blues* and to illustrators Adrienne Smith (cover art) and Nora Hubbard.

Finally to first reader Sharon Laural for keeping the plot 'feelers' in the garden.

Phonetically, my last name is pronounced 'S – pen – shyed'. I believe this information to be important. For the past ten years I've been inspired by Ron Koertge's novels, and I still have no idea how to say his name properly.

PLAYERS

Girl Scout Troop 822

Madison Weber	14, ninth grade
Lily Starr	14, ninth grade
Autumn Hook	13, eighth grade
Rachel Bradbury	13, eighth grade
Ana Story	13, eighth grade
Jessi Bradbury	Scout leader

Town of Sugar City

Dr. Solomon Jolly	physician
Rolli Guy	police chief
Dixie Brackett	librarian

Dry Dog Blues Motorcycle Club

Zeb Story	president
Olin Spoon	
Will Ribbs (Freewheelin')	
Alexander Hamilton (Straydog)	
Robin Emerson	
Harlin Shifter (Rat Tail)	
Gordon Estey (Dimmer)	

Heartland Ironworks Company

Dick Lester	plant supervisor
Paul Weber	finance
Rita Gunsolley	administration

Notables

Judge Cyrus Chute	attorney general's office
Juliet Spinnetti	law student
Kelly Bauer	KBOX-TV summer intern
slacker red	

INTRODUCTION

Directly overhead, from high in the sky, the great white oak plunged earthward. I cupped my ears to smother the piercing screams from allies scattering for their lives. Looking up, torrential rain clogged my nose and mouth. I was laboring for breath, drowning in both water and fear. I stood fixated as the falling oak ripped down through trees still rooted, honing in as if we two were a fated fatal attraction. At the final moment of my life, I cried out, covered my head, and—awoke—sitting up in bed, shaking, drenched in sweat.

Jesus. Not again.

The glow from the table alarm clock read three fifteen a.m. Forcing myself to my feet, I grabbed a fresh night shirt from the dresser drawer and stumbled to the wash basin, flicked the light switch, and doused my head and hair in cold water. Toweling off, I stared at my reflection and winced. Still the same features, all nose and weak chin, now abetted by hollow eyes and sunken cheeks—a gaunt-faced stick from a ration-deprived prison camp. How and why had my existence come to this? Worn ragged at thirty?

The flashbacks are draining me. Maybe I'd better talk to someone—lie on a couch and attempt to explain.

At the county hearing, after sentencing me to a gazillion hours of community service, the judge corralled me afterward, urging that I write it all down. "Give it life, Hamilton. Putting the story to paper might provide a new perspective."

Maybe the old coot was right. Perhaps the time had come. I'll corral the Scoutsters one by one, wade through their OMGs and relate their side as best I can. As for my own tribe, hell, I led the whole way. I'll simply narrate it all first hand.

I added a sweatshirt, still shivering ice cold from the nightmare. I wondered aloud how Weber was making out. Was she up at three, burdened too with guilt and bad dreams?

"You've got remarkable personalities here, Hamilton," the judge had said.

I hadn't seen Weber for months—another huge worry. *Well, here's to you kiddo, and to all the remarkable "rest."* I dug out an old composition book. My hands still twitched from stretching upward to shield my body yet again from the tumbling massive oak tree. I massaged my wrists, seeking calm, then inked a beginning to the short, violent history of—

THE JACKASS ALLIANCE
A SMALL TOWN FABLE

...we swiftly escape as Nature escapes,

. . . .

We become plants, trunks, foliage, roots, bark,

. . . .

We are oaks; we grow in the opening side by side,
We browse, we are...among the wild herds spontaneous as
any...

Walt Whitman
"We Two, How Long We Were Fool'd"

TUESDAY, MAY 1, 2001

Off the east coast of Japan, warm, moist Kuroshio
Current air overtaken by dry air downwind from
the Kunlun Mountain barrier spawns an undetected
midlatitude baroclinic disturbance: the birth of a
maritime polar air mass that, upon maturing May 1st
Greenwich Meridian Time, rumbles east-northeasterly
toward the Gulf of Alaska.

And halfway around the world...

Ripples in the easterly jet above Western Africa south
of the Sahara Desert give birth to a small cluster of
thunderstorms. Trade winds carry the atmospheric
disturbance past cool African coastal waters out into
the warmer Atlantic offshore, growing into a tropical
depression migrating westward toward Cuba.

I
THE LIBRARIAN

"See any 'balls' sitting at this table, Beulah?"

"Land sakes, Dixie, there hasn't been a male librarian in these parts for the past fifty years. Besides, testicles don't sit, they hang."

Dixie, indulging herself over a second schnapps, eyed Beulah and smiled shamelessly. "Sitting, hanging, swinging naked in the breeze, my point being..."

Arladeen butted in. "Girls! Please. Our manners."

Dixie tossed a wave of dismissal. "We're four old biddies." She hesitated. The longtime librarian at Sugar City, Iowa, sat back confused. "Beulah, my train of thought. Where was I?"

Beulah allowed a tender look at her longtime friend. "Balls, biddies, and librarians, dear."

Dixie nodded. "Senior moment. Sorry, girls. Now there's not a young gent nor a junior miss among us, and if we don't find the means to energize our town libraries soon, our undernourished budgets are fixing to turn skin-n-bones. Four libraries in our county, all run by crones ready for pasture." Dixie sighed. "Heaven help us."

The bimonthly meeting of the Hardcastle County Librarians, chaired by Dixie Brackett, was in full swing at Sugar City. It was the first of May and the four were once again in a dogfight over how to wrestle their respective book barns into the twenty-first century. Beulah Cornwall, Mildred Dag, and Arladeen Mueller, who had all driven in from neighboring towns, now looked expectantly at Dixie. Almost in unison they asked, "Well, what are you suggesting this time around?"

"Tarnation, girls. We've got the barns but can't corral the horses. Libraries need to congregate folk. More computers, more space, that's the future. By golly, if I was in my prime, I'd build me one of those new-fangled skateboard parks right next door." Dixie held out her hands, beseeching her friends. "My point being...we're losing our vibrancy, dears. Look at us! Anyone see any Katies, Heathers, Britneys, or Natalies at this table? Names like ours, it's like we all belong on a wagon train."

"You're talking big dollars, Dixie. Nonexistent dollars."

Dixie acknowledged, "I know, I know, Arladeen. But we either join the high-tech march, or risk becoming museums. Gracious, if we can't instill the importance and joy of reading into the coming generation, we're just not doing our job." Dixie slouched. She needed to come down off her pedestal. They had waged this argument many times before.

They settled in together every other month to hash out common victories and defeats alongside a generous snifter and something chocolate. The meetings were never a chore. The four enjoyed each other's company.

"We're getting too bogged down over money and budgets. We need a symbol."

Three faces returned a blank stare. Mildred voiced the obvious, "You've lost me, Dix."

"I'm hazy on this, girls. A symbol that validates." Recently she'd sensed a ghostly presence hovering about. An unseen apparition she perceived as a hopeful sign. She raised her eyebrows. "A key to unlock closed minds."

Beulah couldn't resist. "Another senior moment, Dixie?"

Compact, avocado shaped, gray curls migrating every direction in a perpetual six week-old perm, Dixie Brackett profited from a ruffled countenance that belied the shrewd, robust taskmaster; a role she relished. Her husband, Thomas, had passed on years ago. Her children and grandchildren quartered far from Iowa. Sugar City's library, its survival and growth, had become a personal crusade. Her rasp of a voice alone set her apart. If prunes spoke, they'd sound like Dixanne Brackett. She uncorked an evil eye at her friend. "I find heckling unbecoming, Ms. Cornwall."

"Look Dix," Beulah chided, "we're searching for a pie in the sky here."

"Make that chocolate cream."

"With a spot of brandy."

Amidst the laughter, Dixie said, "I don't mean to sound esoteric, girls, but sometimes my sixth sense kicks in along with my arthritis. We need to stay alert, keep a sharp eye, and maintain an open mind. Our symbol won't be obvious. Let's all think outside the gate. My bones are achin' in the right places.

Hope is near our doorstep. My vision's murky, but mind me... something's out there."

"I believe Dix has been watching too many old *Twilight Zone* episodes," Mildred said with a chuckle.

"More like the *X-Files*," Arladeen added, then said, "Winning lotto ticket be a fine symbol, Dixie."

Dixie shot back, "I don't gamble. A fool's sad search for a shortcut."

Arladeen nodded. "I agree, but when the $160 million check arrives, we'll still split it four ways."

Laughter filled the room.

Beulah slung an arm across her dear friend's shoulders. "Dixie, those skateboarders are going to have a ball."

MONDAY, MAY 7, 2001

A maritime polar air mass, driven by upper level winds, sweeps southeastward down from the Gulf of Alaska, bringing dark, nimbostratus cloud cover and heavy rain to Seattle, Portland, and northern California.

Guided by westward trade winds, an atmospheric disturbance deepens into a tropical depression while crossing the Atlantic. Cuba and Key West brace for gale-force winds packing copious rainfall. Forecasters warn of a possible minor storm surge, flooding, and mudslides, and that the depression could intensify to an early tropical storm upon reaching the warmer Gulf waters.

2
THE IRONWORKS

"How about a skyhook? One of those copter cranes. We pallet up product at shipping and chopper out to a loading site by the highway. Check availability. Try searching 'large-scale construction' in Des Moines. Hell, try the National Guard. They've got all sorts of toys. Christ, Ray, let's not get stuck showing our collective ass. That road fails, I'm not closing shop, goddamn it."

Plant Engineer Ray Conover had a look of dismay. "We can shore it up for a month, maybe two, Mr. Lester, but the more our trucks roll, the worse that mud hole of a pike is going to get. We're damn lucky it's been a dry spring."

"Jesus, a simple rain could shut us down," griped a disgruntled Dick Lester, plant supervisor. He turned to his chief financial officer: "Paul, where are we now?"

Heartland Ironworks (HIW) manufactured continuous fence, feed bunks, corral panels, and custom gates for vendors throughout the upper Midwest. The factory had been built near Wildnut Park, an old-growth grove populated with black,

white, and bur oaks older than the state of Iowa. The grove
dominated the landscape along the Upper Horn River just
outside of Sugar City, Iowa (pop. 2200 souls). It had once been
a favorite picnic spot and Lover's Lane, but the townsfolk had
abandoned it for that purpose when the factory was built in
the nineties.

The factory access ran due north alongside the Upper
Horn River, connecting to State Highway 12. The old, bedded-
rock road was crumbling, slowly becoming part of the Horn
itself. HIW foresaw two options to remedy: go northeast across
the river to the highway or carve out a new road northwest
through Wildnut Park.

Option A necessitated a bridge be built.

Option B was going to fire up the chain saws.

Paul Weber had been dreading this moment. He knew the
decision regarding the road had already been made. These
staff meetings were all smoke and mirrors—top management
going through the motions; Lester acting concerned. What a
sham. Trying to hide any resentment in his voice, he directed
his report. "Plan A is cleared for implementation. State natural
resource reps have approved our bridge site across the Horn.
We have no wetland problem or drainage concerns. Acting
independently, county engineers conclude our new span will
be bedded solid. We've received cost estimates. Not much left
to do but award the contract and let steel and concrete take
shape. Plan B is nearly set. Tree service jobbers have inspected
the grove and provided estimates. Our local removal, Lonnie

Shimmer's outfit, has bid on the project. Either way we choose to go, paving costs for the new road are nearly identical."

Lester broke in. "Cut to the chase, Paul. Ballpark figures: what's this going to run the company?"

"Yes, sir. Cutting through the tree grove saves time plus $500,000 to $550,000." Low soft whistles chorused around the table. "Construction expense for the bridge, a span strong enough to support Transport's semitrucks, stands as the overwhelming cost-differential factor." Paul slid copies of detailed dollar estimates to all present. Despite the air conditioning, he was perspiring. "One item of import, if I may, Mr. Lester."

Stifling impatience, Lester nodded. "Go ahead, Paul."

"Wildnut Park, sir. I'm not sure that it's ours enough to decide the trees' fate. I've been over the land transaction with Sugar City when the plant was first built. Wildnut falls within our jurisdiction, but, and this is somewhat hazy to say the least, any status change to the property requires both parties to be in compliance."

An uneasy silence sat in the meeting room.

Dick Lester cleared his throat. "At ease, Weber. No one's clipping hurtles. Legal in Chicago is well aware our situation."

Paul Weber wouldn't kowtow. Not quite yet. Lots at stake here. He thought of his daughter Madison, and what she'd do.

Paul had relocated south from corporate headquarters in Chicago when the ironwork plant first opened, jumping at the opportunity to cast off the hectic, high-rise, cubicle life to run his own show. The family took a bit more arm twisting. His wife, Betty, was a city gal through and through. Madison had her school and friends. Emotions ran high, tears fell, and in the end they agreed to head down country. Betty bit the bullet hard, but Maddy okayed because she knew the transfer to Iowa was best for Dear Old Dad. Paul doted on his only child. The two of them had always been close. The outgoing girl was heading for places he'd never dreamed. Where had this creature come from? Had there been a distant relative with Magellan—on the Mayflower. He and Betty were, well, ordinary, blend-into-the-woodwork type of folks. He'd stare at the mirror. "This hairline, Betty. This paunch. Let me guess. This guy has got to be an accountant." Betty would laugh almost on cue.

He had given up his boyish dreams years ago. But there was Madison, this incredible gift. "They all follow the money, Pops." Her favorite pick-up-the-old-man line. He was charmed every time. His cute dark-haired, pumpkin-faced kid was a smart girl. When in a quandary, he'd find himself wondering: How would she handle this?

Paul drew a breath to gather his courage. "Understand, sir, I'm no contract lawyer, so let's forgo the fine print. Sugar City coveted our plant. Our location is ideal. Wildnut Park falls within the confines of the town's apportioned industrial acreage, but it's kind of the player-to-be-named-later in the deed purchase. Sugar City's intent was to allow us to act as caretaker and..."

Lester had heard enough, extending his arms, hands outstretched. "Letter of the law? Quasi intent? This is not our call, gents." He'd been appointed plant supervisor a year ago. His stay at Heartland Ironworks was transitory—a corporate grooming position. He knew that. But Sugar City, a five-minute-to-anywhere town, clung to him like an ill-fitting suit with an irritating itch. He felt the head office had jettisoned him to a far flung outpost at the edge of the empire. Quickly he glanced at his watch noting the noon hour. He began to recall past business luncheons in Chicago, those second martinis at Berghoff's—oh yeah—the temper and tempo of life in the Windy City. Now, Christ, wasting away out here in Soybeanburg. Ask for a Beefeaters at a local tavern and all you're going to get is a blank stare. No, wait. There was that young barmaid who took a stab and served up a pickled sausage floating in a glass of Miller Lite. Lester snorted an indulgent chuckle before getting back to the damnable matter at hand. "Our goal right now is to ensure this plant stays up and running. Assume we go the grove route, Weber. How soon might the lumberjacks be set to start?"

Paul grasped that he'd lost big-time. "This is small-town Iowa, sir, just name the day."

Dick Lester stood. "Boys, that's a wrap. Rita, what's the date?"

"Why it's Monday, sir. May 7."

Paul Weber noted that Lester's secretary, poor Ms. Gunsolley, looked, per usual, terrified to be in the same room with her boss. The plant supervisor had a knack for affecting everyone under him with a sense of inadequacy. Natch, Lester had the final say. "Gentlemen, we're going to commence one of our options this Friday. We wait no longer."

TUESDAY, MAY 8, 2001

3
THE TROOP

"Because your inquisition is bugging me, Madison."

"I'm bugging you, Daddy, cause you've been hiding something for awhile and now this something is worse. Me and Mom are worried."

Paul looked up from his dessert seeing Betty with her head cocked as if to say, "Enough, spill it," then back to his fourteen year old personal Grand Inquisitor. "You only call me Daddy when you want something." He sighed. "Look, it's work related...hardly your concern, kiddo."

Madison wasn't sure she could muster up classmate/fellow scout Rachel Bradbury's infamous withering stare, but she gave it her best shot. Across the dining table, her dad appeared to shrink. Maybe it was working. "Whew. Guess we can scratch off gambling debts and the pregnant girlfriend, Mom."

"That's not funny, young lady."

"No, it's not, *Dad*, but if I were acting up, you would be all over me about stressing and keeping things bottled up."

"She's right, Paul."

"Oh, and by the way, Dad, I've a problem at school and got expelled for a couple weeks. Don't know why I'm telling. It's hardly a *concern*."

"Alright alright. Golly, you two are worse than an IRS audit." Paul palm massaged his tired eyes and slowly exhaled. "Here's the deal. I've mentioned our road problems at the plant. Right? Well, construction begins this Friday to layout a new access through old Wildnut Park. Meaning of course, that a lot of the oaks are coming down. It's upsetting to me… whether we've a legal right to alter the park…the loss of the trees…and I've made that point quite clear to Dick and the rest."

"Sorry, Dad."

"Because there's another possible route."

"So take it."

"Because, Madison, it'll require building a bridge and another truckload of money. Plus there's a time factor. The damn road is failing much quicker than anticipated." Paul tossed his napkin in frustration. "The ol' corporate git-er-done is priority one and…there it is. Everyone satisfied?"

"So first they're gonna ax the trees and then ax you?"

"It won't come to that, kiddo, and let me finish that pie you're picking at. Don't you have a Scout meeting tonight?"

"Wait, honey, before you go." Betty was up from the table reaching for her handbag. Digging and finding, she handed over a CD. " One of your classmates dropped by this afternoon with some music. Here you go. He thought you might like this."

"He?"

"Very politely introduced himself. Riley Blue."

Madison flipped the disk back to front, confused. Her dad didn't help matters.

"Why, Miss Weber, I do believe you're being wooed."

"DAD!! I hardly know this...this...guy! Anyway, nobody passes around CDs. Everybody file-shares." It didn't happen often, but her mom had her completely off-guard. "Riley Blue? Why? He was here? At the house?"

Paul Weber saw his chance and snatched the CD from his flustered daughter. "Maybe he's just a shy guy. Hummmm... The Donnas, *get skintight.* Looks very cool. Can I have a listen?"

"Paul! For heaven's sake."

"Wha...I'm too old to be a Donnas fan?"

Madison grabbed it back. "DAD!!" She then kissed him on the cheek and whispered, "Thanks for telling, Pops. I'm late. I'm off."

———

Walking to the church, taking her time, Madison felt a sense of relief. Finally, she knew what had brought Pops so low. Okay, so much for the cause. An idea began to brew— a murky plan taking shape as a way to help. One thing she felt for sure. This mess out at the plant was no small potatoes. He'd been a grouch for too long. *And these trees out at the park—what's the story? Maybe the library be a place to start.* She'd wanted to grill him further, but there at dinner, her mom had so inconveniently changed the subject. The CD-Riley-thing was just too weird. Forget it. But the trees—this was important. This was Dad.

————————

Jessi Bradbury reached down and located the foot-long ruler inside the stuffed paper bag of fiberfill and material remnants she had brought to the Scout meeting. She was relieved they had elected to get together in the early evening. The coolness in the church basement was a respite from the sticky humidity that had clung to the day like a soggy wool blanket. Rapping the wood strip smartly on the work table brought her charges to attention. "Quiet down, girls. Let's get started. Where's Maddy?"

That very moment, Madison Weber was double-timing through the Methodist Church hallway, set to barrel down the stairwell that led down to the Scout den. "Count me in, Mrs. Bradbury," she hollered, skipping down the steps. Madison could hear Lily Starr reciting the Girl Scout Law—from memory, of course.

"I will do my best to be
Honest and fair
Friendly and helpful
Considerate and caring
Courageous and strong"

That girl had a photographic memory, among her many talents. Starr knew everything. Lil the Leonardo. Lil the brainosaur.

MADDY–LILY

They were best friends, having first met two years back seated side by side in seventh grade home room, an encounter that still brought Madison a smile.

"Golly, are you actually reading that?"

Lily rolled her eyes at the monster text weighing down her desk. "Yeah, a novel, *Anna Karenina*."

"I'm Maddy Weber. Why?"

"Hi...Lily Starr." She had long blond hair pulled back around pixie ears. An elf with a slender, pale, lightly freckled face atop a slight frame that conveyed fragility, almost as if the out-of-doors might prove too rigorous. "My mom says it's never too early to start reading the Russian classics. You'll have a leg-up on the Harry Potter generation. Her exact words, for real."

"Your mom sounds a little intense."

"Tell me about it," Lily groaned.

"It's in English, right?"

Lily sighed. "Yes, not that it helps a whole lot with Tolstoy. If you're looking to crack the classics, try Tolkien."

Madison couldn't imagine. She had zero interest but asked anyway, pointing, "What's it about?"

Lily placed her index finger up against her cheek, thought for a moment, and said, "About a woman so in despair over losing her lover that she throws herself in front of a train."

Madison cocked her head, gaining interest. "Wow, I've never even had a boyfriend."

"Me neither, and I'll tell you this, Maddy, after reading *Anna Karenina*, I'm not sure I ever want one!"

Both girls doubled over, laughing.

Their teacher, Norma Hiles, rapped her knuckles atop her desk. "You two in the back settle down. Is that you, Lily Starr? Gracious, what's gotten into you?"

"Yes, ma'am...sorry," Lily answered red-faced. She turned and stared at her new classmate. Who was this strange girl with the Huck Finn grin, flashing her a silly thumbs-up sign as if acting out in class was cool? Ms. Hiles had a point. Then it dawned on Lily. She had told a joke, a good one apparently. That was new. What *had* got into her? Better yet, what was striving to come out?

Reaching her troop, Madison grinned over the recall. Now, in 2001, she and Lil were Scouting Seniors, ninth graders who attended meetings with three younger eighth-grade Cadettes. They were all in attendance tonight: Ana Story, Autumn Hook, and the Scout leader's daughter, Rachel Bradbury. The two troops were miniscule in number. Volunteer adult leaders were at a premium. Joining together made perfect sense.

Lily was wrapping up the Scout Law as Madison plopped on a chair.

"Make the world a better place

And

Be a sister to every Scout"

"Thank you, Lily." Jessi Bradbury eyed her troop. "Priority number one tonight: we need to finalize our summer project. We have to raise money if we want to road trip to the Science Center in Des Moines this fall. Come on, 822. Put your thinking caps on."

"Mom, we could rob a bank."

"Rachel, please, be serious."

Madison chimed in. "Let's pull off the heist in disguise wearing Cub Scout beanies."

Everyone broke up laughing.

"Girls, girls, hey...stop. Something legit. We talked about putting our Scout Law into concrete action and achievement. We've been asked to help out at the assisted care facility. What do you think?" Jessi looked into a small sea of blank faces.

"The museum trip. That's gonna include a mall run, right Mom? A movie?"

"If we can squeeze all that in, hon."

Ana locked arms with Rachel. "Multiplex City. Rock on Mrs. B."

Jessi eyed her daughter and the troop's newest addition, Ana Estrella Story, a charmer great for dropping conversation bombs. The Scouts would be sitting together, learning to hem perhaps, and out of the blue she'd say, "My mom had a dragon tattoo wrapped around her thigh." Everyone would exclaim, "No way!" "Shut up!" Or she'd say, "My *papi* ran a motorcycle club called the Sky Wolves, *Los Lobos del Cielo*." Troop 822 would be aghast, "Whaaa?"

Ana could make their eyeballs grow into full moons. She was petite with light brown skin. Mexican bloodlines provided her broad nose, high cheekbones, and jet-black hair braided into pig tails. At a past meeting over a year ago, they practically tied her to a chair demanding, "Spill it, girl." Ana told her tale.

ANA - RACHEL

"*Papi* and me arrived here from Chula Vista, California. He was a pipefitter at the Navy base nearby, but he spent most of his time with *Los Lobos*. He and this guy Antonio dreamt up the bike club when they were submariners, submerged deep in the Pacific. *Papi* would say, I don't care what we call it, Antonio, but 'sky' has to be in our name. You should have seen my mom, Rene Arandas. So beautiful. *Papi* says she was a total gypsy when they met at some biker-clan-thing. The Sky Wolves were pretty wild. I remember my mom and dad as so romantic. Two years ago everything turned to hell and...sorry, Ms. Bradbury."

"That's okay, sweetie. Tell it your way."

"*Papi* explained to me that what holds together in the military doesn't always work on the outside. The *Lobos* had both American and Mexican guys. Other clubs didn't like that and were always causing trouble, fights and stuff. Then my

THE JACKASS ALLIANCE | 25

mom got fever-sick and there were problems with her green card, like she was an illegal. *Papi* went near crazy trying to keep the peace and take care of her. My mom died. She told us before the end that we must leave, that America was *grande*, that we needed a new place, no more the *combatiente*."

Ana was welling up. All the Scouts were barely breathing.

"I was numb. We had a service. *Papi* stood up and said the club was over for him, that his heart was broken. His family had land in the Midwest. We packed, tied down the Harley on the back of the pickup, and headed east to Iowa. Been over a year now. *Papi* is not the same. He is quieter. He misses the ocean but kinda likes the old farmhouse we inherited. He works with Ora, the Roto-Rooter plumber guy. *Papi* says we went from pipe-fitting to pipe-flushing."

Ana's family-history outpouring made a lasting impression on Rachel Bradbury. She grasped right away their common denominator and post-meeting, sought her out. "We need to talk, Ana. My God, you have an SSP. So do I."

Ana was lost, not comprehending. "An SSP?"

Rachel blurted out, "We've both got single, sad parents."

Ana laughed. "Well, you're right at my end."

Rachel recognized a comrade in arms. "Look, maybe we could like study together or something. It'd be cool to meet your dad."

Ana's eyes lit up. "How 'bout tonight?"

Jessie now thought her daughter and the Californian Ana nearly joined at the hip, but after the heartache Rachel had been through, having a close friend to lean on was a huge plus. She viewed all the Scouts tonight with a satisfied smile. Back in 98, when the district director urged her to head up Troop 822, her first inclination was to shy away. She was glad she eventually changed her mind. The girls were fun, eager, and got along well together. So she became Jessi Bradbury, Scout leader. At least the activities helped keep melancholy at bay. Brian was gone—over three years now. How was that possible? Born to die in a stupid hunting accident. After the sadness came anger. How utterly ridiculous life can be. She harped on herself to leave the enclosing walls of this small town. Change your life, you coward, she'd yell into the mirror. Don't grow old and bitter.

Always in the end, she felt relocating would be unfair to Rachel, to uproot her from school. As for her own dating and forging new relationships, the so-called moving on with life— out of the question. No interest. Maybe she enjoyed wallowing in self-pity as *The Pathetic;* a dubbed name that hurt but fit.

Brian lived on within his daughter. Rachel was a blessing. A mother's daughter; both shared the same fair complexion, delicate facial features, and unruly light-red hair. A beauty, Jessi thought. Me, without sad eyes. Her husband's death drew the two of them close. At times too close. There was a tendency for sorrow. She was glad to see Rachel begin to branch out with the new girl, Ana. *Las dos amigas.* Small-town Rachel grinning with joy over Ana's wild tales of her gypsy mom and being raised by Sky Wolves. Ana, simply luxuriating in the peaceful quiet of rural Sugar City. The two were always conspiring—just like tonight.

"Four minutes at the Science thing, four hours at the mall might get 'er done, right, A?"

"Lots of shops. Big place, R. Maybe three and five be better."

Jessi slapped the ruler to her palm. "Alright, you've had your fun. That's enough you two."

With the troop whooping it up, Ana and Rachel gave each other a happy wink and a high five. Because it wasn't enough. For a year now their grand conspiracy at pushing their mom and dad together had been a struggle. The SSPs were not cooperating. Sisterhood was still a hazy, distant goal. But despite setbacks, they'd had a few victories, like that occasion after a Scout meeting when words were exchanged for the first time ever.

"She should wear a helmet."

He blankly stared right through her, shut down the rumbling Harley, dexterously slid from the saddle, reached back, and retrieved a small skid lid from the bike's leather bags. Ana quickly strapped it on. Next, he ambled over close and with an ever-so-slight smile, simply said, "Thanks for the reminder, Ms. Bradbury." With a nod toward Rachel, he legged back on. The Harley ignited and rumbled off like the Ramones.

"So that's Ana's father."

"What-a-ya think, Mom."

Jessi felt a chill flutter throughout her body. She knew the sensation wasn't fear, more like a...what? A confusion.

Then there was that post office thing:

"Hope you're raising my daughter well."

Zeb smiled. "Let's just say that if Ana turns to drugs and crime, she and Rachel will share bunks in the slammer together."

"Not funny, Mr. Story."

"Sorry. Meant it to be. And the names Zeb. Feel free to use it."

"Why?"

Zeb leaned in and took a step closer. "Because, Ms. Bradbury, the 'Mr.' might construe I'm a generation older than you and that's not only untrue, it's unfair."

Jessi took a step back. He was too close. "Our daughters have become inseparable. I was only being polite. And you do the same. I don't need an older age bracket myself."

Playfully squabbling over who was younger broke the ice as they engaged at last in small talk that proved natural and relaxed, surprising both of them. As she collected her mail and began to leave, Zeb doffed his ragged Padres baseball cap, smiled, and said, "Good day, Jessi." She returned the gesture, only the Cub logo was different.

And then there was the mortifying sleepover gaffe:

"You should date my mom, Mr. Story. We've taken showers together. I can vouch for her. She's hot."

Zeb stared flabbergasted.

Ana barely stifled a burst of laughter. "Rach...God!"

Zeb collected himself, cleared his throat. Laughing along with Ana probably wouldn't be appropriate.

Rachel caught his stern gaze. "Sorry, Mr. Story. I was just wondering if you'd taken any notice?"

"Must be the times we live in," Zeb declared, deftly side-stepping Rachel's curiosity. "All this provocative music and movies. You know, Rachel, there are times I wish we'd return to the Victorian Age."

"What's that, Mr. Z?"

"I'll tell you, kiddo. An age when all was prim and proper. When young ladies," Zeb eyeballed both girls intently, "did not encourage a potential suitor by implying that their mom was 'hot' in the shower."

Chagrined, Rachel mustered, "Oops. Sorry I crossed the line."

"Your mom's a beautiful woman, Rachel. That should answer your question. Now you two schemers get some sleep."

Rachel was quick to add, "She doesn't show it much anymore, but she used to laugh out loud a whole bunch."

Zeb grinned. "I'll try my best knock-knock joke next time we meet."

"Can I ask you a question, Mr. Story?"

"Shoot."

Rachel hesitated, then took a plunge. "Do you hunt?"

"Only for my car keys, Rachel."

"Good."

Couldn't the SSP's see they were perfect for one another? Rachel and Ana found it unfathomable that both their parents were blind as bats.

"My mom suggested pot holders," Autumn Hook pitched in, corralling the Scout meeting back on track. "Maybe we could stitch 'em together and sell them to stores all over town, even the grocery."

Jessi turned enthusiastic. "Now there's a great idea, Auti. They are relatively easy to make and everyone could use a second pair. We might even go door-to..."

"How about a troop protest?" Madison Weber butted in. "Girl Scout Power. Like the sixties."

Jessi's alarm bells began ringing. Weber's schemes did that. "Protest what, Maddy?"

Madison paused and thought, *Wow, that was sorta quick. What am I doing? Best keep Pops out of the loop.* "Ahhh, Ms. Bradbury, rumor has it the old oaks are going to be cut down over at Wildnut Park."

"What?"

"Yeah, a road's being built. Through the trees!"

"Gracious, how did you hear this? Are you certain?"

Again Madison took a moment. She was winging it. "Squirrels told me?"

"Look, hon, protesting is hardly the type of activity our troop commits to. If I might ask your squirrel, when is this all supposed to occur?"

"This weekend starting Friday. We need to stop 'em from taking the trees."

"Sweetheart, this is way beyond Scouting."

"But Ms. Bradbury."

Jessi was befuddled. "I share your concern, Maddy. I'll ask questions. I'll make an inquiry around town, okay?"

Madison nodded. It was a start. "Sure, but I don't think an inquiry is going to keep them safe."

"I promise, Maddy. I'll find out what's going on." Jessi looked to the rest of the girls. "Can we switch the subject back to potholders? I believe Autumn's idea is super. Everyone needs to think about style and design. Let's map out a plan to get production up and rolling."

Later, Jessi left to procure juice and snacks from the church kitchen. Madison had her chance, whispering, "Listen up guys, before she returns. Are you with me on this tree thing? We gotta make up some signs and figure out how to use 'em. Maybe at the park. Think about it tonight, okay?"

Autumn, Lily, Rachel, and Ana looked confused but nodded in agreement anyway.

Madison was rushing. "Don't tell anyone. Let's meet tomorrow in school, at lunch, outside. I'll explain better. We gotta do something, guys. I mean it! You okay with this, Rachel? I don't want to get you in trouble with your mom."

Rachel gave Madison a squinty-eyed, scornful look. "Yeah, right." She sat back and slumped down. "Mum's the word, Spiderwoman, but let me remind everyone here that when she saddles up on her high horse, 'Trouble' is Weber's middle name."

Jessi was oblivious to the conspiracy afoot amongst the troops. As they were gathering belongings and getting set to go, she nonchalantly asked, "Oh Ana, by the way, could you um...check with your dad? We're having a terrible drain problem at the house. Just cropped up everywhere. Bath. Kitchen. Perhaps he might schedule us in and stop by to take a look."

Ana shot Rachel a look, their eyes registering *Bingo!* as she quickly answered, "Absolutely, Ms. Bradbury. I'll get *Papi* on it right away. He'll come and clean your pipe."

Everyone stopped what they were doing and stood shock-still. Attempting to hold back a burst of laughter, Autumn snorted so hard, snot shot from her nose. Madison had her hands clamped against her mouth. Rachel stared disbelieving, crackling, "Oh my God, Ana!"

Ana, her faux pas now registering, felt blood rush to her head. "Gosh, sorry, Ms. Bradbury."

Jessi turned barn-red and made an attempt to salvage an already lost situation. "Girls, please. Get your minds out of the gutter."

Naturally, any reference to pipes and drains hardly helped and produced another uproar. Even perpetrator Ana was grinning.

Above the lighthearted mayhem stood Lily. There's always got to be one. "Hey, everyone stop, just stop," she shouted. "What's so funny? I hate this. I don't get it."

The merriment all around was now infectious. Even Jessi could no longer hold back and joined in the silliness.

Rachel took a quick, short breath. Startled. She hadn't heard her mom really laugh in a long, long time.

WEDNESDAY, MAY 9, 2001

Calling their forecast a "spring skiers delight," local meteorologists in Denver predict a foot of snow at Arapaho and Loveland Basin. The slow-moving cold front and accompanying high winds could produce near-blizzard conditions at higher elevations from Missoula to Colorado Springs before racing eastward toward the western prairie.

Tropical storm Adrienne, packing winds of forty-five mph, blew ashore on the Texas-Louisiana border. Spiral rain bands produced heavy downpours. Little wind damage was reported. Metro forecasters for Houston and Austin were joyfully anticipating rain-dancing in the streets for most of parched southern Texas. Flash flood warnings have been posted throughout the region. The National Weather Service reports Adrienne is expected to spread westward toward the Marfa front and expand northward, entering the southern plain states Thursday, May 10 and Friday, May 11.

4
THE TROOP

"The trees over at Wildnut, you say."

"Yes um, like a history or anything like that."

"Haven't you got a class that needs attending at school?"

"I've got a free period study hall this morning. Miss Rose is out sick sudden. Here's my permission slip."

Dixie Brackett gave the note a cursory look. "You haven't much time, Madison. This important enough to come a runnin' over here?"

"Yes um. Kinda."

"The old oaks."

"Yes um."

"Follow me, young lady."

Dixie stood up from behind her cluttered desk and led Madison to the rare periodicals room. Scanning book shelves housing county histories, genealogy magazines, yellowed newspaper, pioneer family histories and the like, she found the volume she was looking for: Hardcastle County and It's Peoples 1836-1915. Alone in the library, the two sat at a long study table.

"Want to show you this. It's a favorite."

Dixie thumbed through pages then slid the open book over and Madison found herself peering at a full-page black and white photograph.

"Those folks you're looking at are the Biesemeyers, all gathered at the park—wedding or anniversary reception probably. Don't believe it was called Wildnut back then. Hardly matters, but gander at that car they're surrounding. That's a 1904 Oldsmobile Curved Dash…and that automobile, Madison, was the first four-wheeled petrol contraption to ever stir up the dusty trails about Sugar City."

"Wow."

"Quite a conversation piece it was, I'm sure, and knowing Sugar like I do, I'm positive too that everyone had a high minded opinion as to it's proper place and future." She chuckled. "Now, what else do you see there?"

"The trees."

"The very same, Madison. Fact is, you and I can scoot out to the park this very afternoon and find ourselves at the exact spot the photographer stood…when…ninety seven years ago."

Madison could not take her eyes from the picture. "They were full grown even back then. Golly, Mrs. Brackett, how old are they?"

"Hard tellin', but oaks take a goodly spell to reach maturity. If I told you they were sprouting alongside Abraham Lincoln, I reckon that would be a close guess." Dixie gave the girl a skeptical look. "What's all the interest? Some sort of school report?"

As she had with Rachel's mom, Madison turned hesitant. Her half baked plans were best left secret—at least for now. "Ahh—Scouts, Mrs. Brackett. Nature walk thing. Just wanted to know what I'm gonna be looking at." She pointed at the photo. "Those trees have more stories behind 'em?"

Dixie sensed the teenager was dancing about. "Scout walk. Good for you. Glad you've taken an interest, hon," She raised an eyebrow, "for whatever reason. Now then, to answer your question. Not so much a story, but we've a few minutes and I'd like to add some."

"Sure."

"First off, the trees are sure-as-shootin' the oldest living inhabitants in and around Sugar City. Why, they've held sway over this town's entire existence…and it's nice to have that. You are just beginning your life, Madison, and I'm certain you've far flung dreams in the making, so what I'm about to say probably won't make too much sense right now. But listen," Dixie provided Madison a meaningful look. "We all need to be grounded in some way—secure to a place or thing that ties everything together." She smiled. "A place to hang all the hats if you catch my drift. Might be a homestead. Heck, could be an old baseball park and team…even an old tree grove. Am I making any sense here?"

Madison cocked her head. "Some."

"Good, because if someone doesn't tighten the reins, my age bracket gets to meandering into nonsense. Maybe I'm saying that some things in life are vital even though we take them for granted day to day. We just expect them to be there for us cause they've always been there…an anchor…a gift…and that's quite enough from me. Time for you to scoot back."

Madison jumped up and checked her watch. She hadn't far to walk. The public library was just across the street from the school. "Are there more books and pictures to check out, like after classes?"

"You and I could get to diggin'. We've got these archives plus the internet. Might be fun."

Madison nodded. "Thanks, Mrs. Brackett. See you at three."

———————

At noon, five Scouts met outside as planned during lunch hour at school. Grabbing a remote cement table shaded from the hot sun, Madison Weber laid out her plan and asked straight out, "Are we gonna do this? Can we do this?"

Lily frowned. "Skipping school! Lying to my parents! You're asking a lot, Madd."

Ana nodded in agreement. "Is this *rebelión* really worth the stress? We'll all wind up in detention for sure. I'm with Lil. *Papi* might ground me for life."

"Like total social purgatory," Rachel added, as if dotting the exclamation point.

Madison grew a lump in her throat. They were right. She was asking way too much. Staring at four questioning faces, she chided herself to be honest with them. "I guess I was thinking only of my dad. He's the one who told me that the trees had to be wiped out to build a stupid road. He's been in a funk about the park. Said for a few more bucks they could build a bridge and go a different way. And for real I'm finding out the trees are sorta super special. I wanted to help. I wasn't worrying about you guys. Sorry."

Rachel shook her head. "Typical Madd. Damn the tornadoes, full speed ahead."

There were a few snickers as the girls sat with their thoughts. Lily ventured, "That's 'Man the torpedoes,' not..."

She got the Rachel *look*. "Whatever."

Autumn had heard enough. "Way I see it is we're all out there for a couple hours. We'll have signs. Make a ruckus. Try to stop 'em, and be back in class before third hour. What's the big deal?"

Madison looked gratefully at the tall, willowy blond. Autumn's willingness to help might sway the rest of the troop. She was an impact girl. Statuswise, Scouting was not considered a must-do activity with the in crowd at Sugar City High. On the contrary, wearing the khaki suit at fourteen was pretty much in the lame bin. But athletic Autumn being a 822er lent the humble outfit considerable cred on the sliding cool scale.

Autumn Hook was a legend in the making within Sugar City. There was a weight of expectation on her slender shoulders. A weight that was essentially unfair. Her older sister, Summer, had led the Sugar City High class one-A basketball team to the state tourney three years prior. Never before had any Redhawk sport team, boys' or girls', stormed such heights. Within the confines of their small burg, Summer and her teammates, reverently dubbed the Scream Team, achieved mythical status. As fate would have it, Madison Weber had been the team ballgirl back then in the winter of 97, and as such was center stage as Summer Hook rose to stardom. Autumn, alike in physique with matching skills, was preordained by town folk to lead the Redhawks to greater glory. Now that her own time had come, she was wont to confide in Madison. Worried. *Basketball's just a game, isn't it?*

Madison glanced wearily at her friends. "Look at it this way guys, one of us isn't gonna change anything but the five of us could be a major force." She waited expectantly. Perhaps they might yet band together to save the old oaks. They sat. No one volunteered a count-me-in.

Rachel eyed both Autumn and Madison. She was aware of the link between the two of them. "What you're arm-twisting us to do isn't like a basketball game, Maddy. Who's going to support us?"

"Right now, no one."

Ana spoke up, "What's all this stuff about basketball?"

"Tell her, Madd," Lily said. "Ana wasn't around for the Redhawk Senior Scream Team. When was that? Three years ago? Tell the story."

"Don't have to," Madison said matter-of-factly. "In a couple of years Autumn will emerge the unstoppable Amazon and more than match her sister's success. Ana can watch the games for real."

"Yeah, *right*," Autumn offered, straining for all the sarcasm she could muster.

"Guys...forget basketball," Maddy pleaded. "No, wait. Maybe there's a connection. Five on the team. Five of us. Fives rule! Our cause is just!"

"So was Davito Crockett's," Ana deadpanned. "And a lot of good it did him."

Madison countered. "We're hardly going to be overrun by an army, Ana."

"That's just the point," Rachel cried out. "You don't know that. Our butting-in over at Wildnut is not a school function with alums and boosters. The basketball team has a coach. Our coach is my mom and we all know where she stands on this."

Madison was losing them, and why not? The whole scheme was nuts to begin with. She was on the ropes, one stiff jab away from tossing in the towel. "Your mom's pitching in, Rach. She's making calls."

"Not the same, Webslinger."

Stalemate hovered over Troop 822.

Lily tried again. "Following the footsteps of an older sister has got to be hard. And don't forget, Ana's in the dark with this basketball thing. Besides, Madd, I'm your best friend and even I only know bits and pieces. Tell the story. Right, guys?"

Madison glanced around the table. Ana sat expectantly. The rest were nodding, offering consent. "We got time? Everyone okay with this?"

Watches were checked. A near-communal reply followed. "Sure."

"Do we have a choice?"

"Rach!"

"Just teasing, Maddy. I've never heard the whole 'B-ball tale' either."

Madison relaxed and backtracked four years. "I had volunteered on a whim to be manager for the high school team. I was eleven, new in town, and no one else wanted the job. I was supposed to be the coach's assistant or something. Yeah, coach's aide my butt! I was more like chief towel fetcher. But hangin' with seniors was cool. You guys remember them? For starters there were the Brinkerhoff twins."

"Golly, like huge."

"Yeah, Auti. Farm girl tough. Definitely. Really nice though 'cept if there was a rebound to be had. Clank. Here they come. Get out of the way. Then your Summer sister, of course, the star ta da. Also roadrunner Tess, and that Vietnamese girl, Soramy...and coach Zaro to be sure. We called her Slash. Anyway, Ana, that was the team and they were playing kinda drippy. Finally, after another bungled loss, like for the first time ever, coach went bonkers."

"Know what's been our problem all season? We're too dang nice to each other...and don't you dare look at me confused. Let me spell it out for you. You're all too concerned about giving everyone a chance. Making that extra pass, passing up shots...I'm looking at you, Summer...to make sure we all somehow share the glory...and please, let me be the first to point out that there is not much glory to be shared, not the way we've been playing."

Tess Pepper spoke up. "So, Coach Z, we got problems. Where's our comeback?"

Pepper's question was just what Margo hoped for. "Okay, here goes. From now on everyone will play only to their strengths. Each of you will have a strict role to fulfill on the court. On offense, we'll draw up four plays and run them to perfection. No more improvising. No more Miss Congeniality contests. Questions? Comments?"

Margo let her stump speech sink in. The locker room was library quiet. Madison, standing off to the side, broke the silence. "Sounds like the dwarfs are finally ditchin' Snow White."

Whoops, hoots, and gales of laughter drowned out the clattering locker room heat pipes. Rolling her eyes, smiling, Margo got specific. "Okay. We have two shooters: Soramy and Summer. Tess 'feeds' and the B's crash the boards. From here on out all our plays are geared with those strengths in mind." She drew back, wanting more than robots on the court. "Now this doesn't mean that Tess and Billie can't take a shot if and when opportunities arise. I don't want us in complete lock step..."

"How 'bout me, coach?" A voice piped up as her teammates roared with delight. Besides an occasional put-back, Bobbie Brinkerhoff treated the ball in her hands like a radioactive moon rock. Her sister Billie was a pretty good shotmaker, but Bobbie was born ham-fisted.

Margo reached out and affectionately tousled Bobbie's hair. God, she loved these kids. "Look," she implored, "let's just pump ourselves up with what we each do best."

"It all worked. We got hot at the end and going to State all came down to that final game at Wheatfield. You gotta know, Ana, in our corner of the globe, Wheatfield never loses." Madison felt the present fade and drifted back to that crazy night from four years past.

Slash's Redhawks were at their best but found themselves twelve down at the start of the fourth quarter. The Wheatfield Wreckers were flat-out tough. That's when a bout of loutish behavior turned fortune's wheel.

Both teams, as usual, were being ardently supported by their male counterparts. The boys' painted faces and get-ups were outrageous and fun. With the Wreckers out in front the entire game, Johnny Ray Briggs and a few Wheatfield cronies had been racing out to the parking lot between quarters to chug beers. One too many, history will relate. With both teams resting and receiving final instructions before play resumed, shit-faced Johnny Ray began hollering at the Redhawks:

"Hey you Sugar City Cup Cakes...

You ain't gonna make it. Too many sweet rolls!

Your butts are draggin', hot buns!

Yo, twinskies, too many Twinkies!

Hey chocolate cherr..."

Brigg's drunken taunt kept on as those seated close by lunged to shut him up. But the damage was done. Yelling frustration at the refs and good-natured trash-talk were common at games, but out-and-out embarrassing the girls was crude and unforgivable.

Madison remembered the girls' faces being as red as their uniforms. Margo thought they were ready to climb into a shell and crawl back home. But the blood rushing to the head of Tess and her teammates was from anger, not humiliation. They silently and steadfastly eyed one another, nodded, jogged to center court and proceeded to play possessed.

Nearing game's end in that wild fourth quarter, the Redhawks signaled for a time-out. They were down two with eight seconds remaining on the scorer's clock. Margo mapped out the final play. Nothing fancy. Tess would cross center court and look for Summer near the foul line behind a Brinkerhoff double screen.

"If it's not there," Margo encouraged Tess, "find Soramy in the corner. Take the three, Amy. Go for the win. Hands together, Redhawks. Heads and hearts!"

Nothing worked as planned.

Tess controlled the ball on a great inbound pass from Soramy, but Summer tripped over a Wheatfield player making her way out toward the Brinkerhoff line. Billie and Bobbie saw her fall and panicked; running opposite directions. With Summer down the Wreckers doubled up on Soramy. Tess was hip-shaking left-right-left, working hard to get past her opposing guard. The clock was ticking. She heard fans on both sides count down. With no shot of her own in the making, other than a desperation heave, she spotted out of the corner of her eye an open red shirt, and flung the rock.

The open Redhawk was stunned and terrified to find herself at the receiving end of Pepper's bullet pass. Grabbing hold—the crowd screaming "ONE!"—B launched a shot at the bucket.

Everyone remembers the moment as if time suddenly slowed. Everyone recalls watching the ball's flight, while simultaneously leaning over to the person sitting next to them to ask which twin took the shot. With Billie, they all knew there was chance for a minor miracle.

The tension-drenched Sugar City faithful stood as one, praying with fingers crossed. The ball's flight from three-point range was hardly a floating lazy arch; more like a flat laser beam. History will record that with the final buzzer sounding, Bobbie's shot hit the backboard like Dale Jr. careening off the wall at Talladega. For Bobbie didn't just throw it. Her effort was more a one-handed-fingertip-hard-push that cut through the stagnant gymnasium air, whirling with backspin. In a nanosecond the basketball ricocheted off the glass and through the net like an NBA jam-slam. So fast did the ball rip through, for a few moments the packed field house lay dead silent. Then—complete bedlam.

Later, rehashing the wonder-of-it-all, Bobbie recalled falling to her knees after releasing the shot. Suddenly this wild herd of arms, legs, and long hair was hurtling toward her.

Sister Billie, eyes alight, was the first to reach her. The rest
piled on. Bobbie laughed. "The only comparable scene was
years ago choring in the sty. Papa drove by. The old flatbed
backfired and stampeded the hogs. Both times...buried!"

The Sugar City Redhawks (at long last)—State tourney
bound regional champs.

Johnny Ray Briggs (Lord bless him)—exiled forever in
teenage wasteland.

Having spun her tale, Madison took a breather, sitting
back, arms crossed against her chest. Wow. She was amazed.
It had all come back so quickly and easily. Then Rachel, of all
people, kept her going by asking, "What about State and that
red carpet thing?"

She sat back up slapping her forehead. "Oh yeah, no one
expected much. First-time tourney qualifiers are usually easy
pickings for the experienced teams. Everybody was so nervous
playing in that huge arena in front of all those people. Every
day Slash had them repeating: *We're just as good as anyone else.*
Then wow, we won that opening game. Summer scored like
forty points or something. She was awesome."

Autumn clapped her hands in delight. "I was there!
Screamed till I was totally hoarse."

"Everybody did. We became the crowd favorite. Then,
well...we kinda fizzled in the next one. Heading home that
night; no one on the team, not me, not even Coach Zaro, had
a clue what was coming...only Louie, the bus driver. At first we
were kinda glum riding back. Well...not everyone. Slash was

totally upbeat and kept riding us to cheer up. And coach was right. The whole tourney had been pretty cool. But nobody, Rach, and I mean *nobody* was prepared for Sugar City's salute. Louie shouted from his driver's seat about some detour up ahead so we pulled off and took the old county road home. From a mile out, you could see the lights. I swear, hundreds of cars and pick-ups from town were parked on both sides of that final stretch, lights beaming. The road looked like a carpet of gold. They had search lights hooked up. Beams of white light circled the night sky. A lot of folks were standing atop their wheels, cheering. It was crazy. As Louie crept along, we were like totally amazed. Then Tess pulled down her window and started screaming and waving with the best of them. The whole bus followed suit, everyone clapping and hollering, stamping their feet. *So* awesome."

"Thanks for telling the story, Madison."

"For sure, Ana. I love remembering that time."

"Not to be a nerd, but we got to get back to class."

"Hold on, Lil," Rachel said, "there's still time before the late bell. Funny, don't you guys think, how this town can come together if they put their minds to it."

Ana wasn't set to change the subject, her mind still abuzz over the Redhawks. "Ms. Zaro died, didn't she?"

Rachel frowned. "Gosh Ana, I don't think Maddy needs to talk about that."

Madison shook her head. "That's okay, guys. Coach Z had cancer. Never told any of us. She died that very fall, in 98. I'd never lost anyone close."

"Summer cried for weeks," Autumn said. "Never saw my sister in such a state. Our dad talked to us after the funeral. He said that there are times people set foot in our lives and make a huge impact, but for any number of reasons, we can't hold on to them. Then they're gone, but hearts don't forget the important stuff."

The girls were quiet for a spell. Then Autumn leaned in close, her eyes sparkling. "Hey Troop. Listen up. I've got us a plan for Friday."

Hook's bomb jolted the Scouts back to the decision at hand.

"Whoa."

"Plan?"

"Give, girl."

"Okay, here goes." Autumn was chomping at the bit to spring her scheme, talking a mile a minute. "I've an overnight planned at my gramps's for Thursday. He's got that farm near the Heartland factory. On Friday morning, like at dawn, you guys gather at the south end of Chestnut with all the gear, signs, and stuff. I'll pick you up with grandpa's old Ford truck and we'll drive out to the park. How's about we meet at six a.m.? That early, that part of town, no one will be around. Piece of cake."

The girls were stunned and spooked. None of them had even agreed in principle to Madison's crazy scheme.

Rachel: "You know how to drive a truck?"

Ana: "You're going to heist your grandpapi's *camion*?

Autumn laughed. "Guys, guys, come on. We're just borrowing, and my gramps taught me to drive around the farm years ago. The old thing has no key, just a choke and push-start on the floor. It's stashed at the abandoned barn far from the house. Gramps will be checking on calves. He won't know a thing. No problem. What do you say, Madd?"

Lily moaned in disbelief, "Oh, this is just great. We've got a stolen truck, an underage chauffeur behind the wheel with dubious driving skills...we're skipping school...uhhh...lying as to our whereabouts...it's all...it's all...somebody give me a word?"

"Unprecedented."

"Exactly. Thank you, Rachel"

"And while we're at it," Rachel clapped her hands, "we better kidnap the boys' wrestling team and pick up a couple of six-packs. No sense going half-way with this thing."

Laughter and high-fives bought Madison time. She gulped, never really believing they'd back her. Now, here they sat—with plans. She imagined herself in the middle of a high dive, wondering how deep the water was below. Plans and talk were one thing, but actions get kind of scary. "Before we agree to anything, we need a vote. Lily's right. This is more complicated than *no problemo.* On Friday we wear our vests. Anyone out and about will see it as a Scout thing."

Lily was despondent. "It is a Scout deal, Maddy."

"Sorry, Lil. You're so right. I'm scatterbrained here." Madison felt her face redden. "Look, we'll all be together. We'll be safe." Madison turned away from Lily's skeptical gaze. "And everyone...stuff a water bottle in your backpack. Supposed to stay icky warm. I mean...if we agree on anything."

"We need more than water and protest signs," Rachel said. "We need to win. We have to somehow stop the tree cutters. Who will help us? My mom can call and complain, but it'll be too little, too late. Who's on Heartland's side? The cops? The mayor?" Rachel had a forlorn look. "I mean, standing around with a bunch of stupid signs watching the trees chopped is going to be awful."

Four sets of expectant eyes shook Madison's composure. She had no plan of action. Rachel was so on target. They'd be in big trouble for nothing. "Kinda grim, huh? I do sorta know one guy who might help. It's Wednesday. We have tomorrow. I guess we don't have to decide now."

"*Yes, we do!*"

"*Amigas,* listen. Why can't we be scream-team, part two?" Ana asked with a conspiratorial wink. "If Autumn's ready to rock, me too."

Rachel said, "I've done nuttier things. Maybe. Come on troop, hands together."

With mischief shining in their eyes, they all slowly looked to Lily.

"Oh right, like I've got a choice." She extended slender arms. "Can't believe we're doing this."

Ten young hands went searching for a companion, found one, and held on tight.

THE DRY DOG BLUES

5
THE BLUES

Zeb Story swung the old gavel down hard. Too hard. With
a resounding *thwack*, the wooden head shattered from its
handle, ricocheted off the table, sliced through the air, and
smacked Harlin Shifter upside the forehead.

"Damn Story, what the hell? Shit, man."

Zeb grinned, holding the headless handle that now looked
like a tiny whiskbroom.

"Whatever it takes, Harlin, to bring this mob to order."

Mob? Not quite. The Dry Dog Blues is a local motorcycle
club, six guys who collectively would have hardly known one
another if not for the machines they rode. The club exists
thanks to me. Alexander Hamilton's the name. I know—rings
a bell. Mother taught American History. Having a maiden
name like Fricke provided little recourse for her, but when
she married a Hamilton and conceived a son, she leapt at
the opportunity. Being named for a Founding Father is
not an albatross. I actually take pride in shouldering the
moniker. And mother always advised, "You can tell a lot about

an individual in how they react." Case in point, the lout at a party who scoffs, "The guy with the kite, right?" Enough said. If there's a downside, it's personal. Alex H. circa 1776 accomplished so much early on in life...and I'm still trying to get mine kick started. Comparisons can be discouraging.

Anyway, putting together a bike club had been a longtime dream of mine. Zeb Story was the catalyst. I pestered Zeb after he and his daughter Ana moved to town until he grew so sick of me whining, "Hey, we got to do this," that he finally caved. Shifter and Spoon joined right away. Later on, Ribbs and Estey filled our six-man roster.

Shattering the gavel had all of us at attention. The Blues had existed for about a year. We're an odd bunch, but we've got the right guy in charge. Everything about Zeb Story is expansive. Gals might peg him Clark Gable handsome. The man radiates a quiet intensity, the kind of guy who's a presence without being beefy or tall. You know the type. Kid goes out for football. Coach dismisses him as too lightweight. Halfway through the season he's the linebacker at the bottom of every pile. That's Zeb Story.

To be honest, we aren't much of a club. Every ten days or so during the summer we put our collective heads and skinned knuckles together to keep the machines rolling. We ride to local motorcycle rallies in Illinois, Missouri, and Iowa, camp out, down some brews. Easygoing stuff.

Last summer, on a fine, sunny morning, we were headed southwestward toward Nine Eagles State Park. We had

Spoony's rickety van stocked with food, beer, and bedrolls. State troopers pulled us over for a fuse-blown headlight. Shifter's handlebar ape hangers probably didn't help. Even together the two minor harassment-type infractions were hardly cause for a search. But then someone's (ahem) small bag of ditch weed turned up, and with that, the cops confiscated the van. "Beyond pissed" doesn't come close to our reaction. One of the troopers actually drew his shotgun and said with a sneer, "Looks like you boys are gonna be dry dogs this weekend." Overzealous nitwit. We ended up with a ruined run, but at least the smokey was kind enough to name our outfit. The Dry Dog Blues Motorcycle Club was born.

"All right! All right, settle down, dammit," Zeb bellowed. "We'll shoot straight to new business and take the vote."

Our *new business* was standing off to the side looking like a lost hen in a wolf den. A new member to be voted on. One Ms. Robin Monnington Emerson: married, mother of two, tall, lean, athletic, and attractive. Her husband Wayne was a chief's deputy in town, a fact that was not, according to Harlin Shifter, her best feature.

"Robin, quit standing there holding up the building and grab a seat at the table. Make some room, Hamilton. It's been a spell since we voted Estey in. So, as a reminder, we do this honorably. Voice vote. No sacred-creed-secret bullshit. Two votes against and the candidate is denied. Where's Ribbs?"

Spoony answered. "Said he might be held up at the work, not to wait."

Zeb nodded. "We're enough. We need a nomination and a second from the floor. But before we get to Robin," Zeb's shoulders drooped, "I want to once more castigate the low-life who keeps liberating beers from the club fridge without paying. For those who can't read, the sign says a buck a brew. Every damn meeting we're outta beer and short on resupply cash."

Shifter spat, "One of these days we're gonna catch your thievin' butt, Dimmer. Look at ya, body all bloated on Buds."

Gordon 'Dimmer' Estey sat shocked. "Wasn't me, Harlin. Honest."

In truth, Estey *is* a butterball. His initials, G. E., might have earned him the nickname "Tower of Light." At Sugar City High, Gordon was the football team's offensive line three years running. But no one ever tagged this naive gentle giant for Stanford. Protecting quarterbacks was his talent. Math, history, science, and English made little impact. Post-graduation, as the years sped by, he nosedived from gridiron hero to forgotten jackstraw. The Tower of Light became Dimmer, and the name stuck. There was a smoothness about him, similar to those athletes who combine a huge physique with soft hands and a graceful manner. But girls had missed him somehow. In that hurtful manner that coils in the corners of American high schools, he unfairly got shelved as slow, a bit retarded.

Olin Spoon and Harlin Shifter befriended him. Spoony had an old battered Honda Goldwing gathering dust. Shifter joked that Dimmer was born to ride. The three of them stitched the bike back together, added heavy duty shocks, and got her running. Estey was overjoyed to join the Dry Dog Blues, and Shifter found himself with an occasional sidekick and useful foil.

Having spent his life in Sugar City, Estey was a fixture—a rarely viewed painting still hanging on the wall—that city maintenance guy. Few took the time or interest to get to know him personally. He could be useful. In Shifter's hands, Estey was like molding clay. Prime example: Shifter wanted Robin Emerson turned away from his world. Gordon Estey could make that happen.

Zeb eyed Shifter. "Let's not be calling the kettle black, eh Rat Tail."

Shifter returned the stare. "You got no cause, Story."

"Yeah right," Zeb laughed. "For the last time, we're on the honor roll. Freeloading suds a capital crime. Enough shenanigans. We've got a prospect."

Olin Spoon shot an arm upward. "I'm one of Ms. Emerson's sponsors and I gladly submit her name for membership."

If we're a bunch of odd ducks, Spoony fits the bill. He's seventy years young for starters. An amicable gent with square-jawed, matinee good looks aided by an unruly mop of charcoal gray hair that hasn't seen a stylist since the Beatles came ashore. A widower, he'd joined the Blues more for company than anything else. He rides a 64 R650 Beemer and tinkers expertly on vintage euro BSAs and Triumphs. "I've a passion for raising the dead," he'd say. A retired engineer at John Deere, Olin's a crackerjack mechanic. Any motorcycle club would kill to have him.

Nodding at Spoon, I quickly seconded.

"Discussion," Zeb directed. "Let's keep it decent for a change. All candidates have the right to be present when voted on if they so desire. Robin has chosen that right. We'll start with you, Olin."

"What's to discuss? She owns a Sportster. She's a fine motorcyclist, born and bred Sugar-Cityite, she's alive and breathing, and she'll add beauty to the beast. We're blessed to have her."

I needed to get my two cents in. "Robin's got spunk. Takes backbone to break the gender barrier in the Blues. She'll make the whole club more...what's the word here...agreeable."

"Agreeable to who?" Shifter grumbled. "I say we vote her down."

"I believe proper grammar calls for *agreeable to whom,*" Spoon corrected.

"How 'bout we vote you out too, Dr. Webster?"

Olin sat suppressing a grin. "I believe I'm tenured."

"Grounds, Shifter," Zeb contested with a wink at Spoon, "better be good."

"Whole idea of gals in the club rubs me raw," Harlin said. "This ain't the Harley Owners Group. If she's such a joiner, her butt belongs in HOG. We ain't the AMA neither."

Harlin Shifter, the prototype loner, asks for no quarter and gives none. Lots of guys are holiday biker warriors— investment banker Monday through Friday, Marlon Brando on the weekend—but Shifter's the real McCoy. His FLH 76 Shovelhead defines him. Harlin rides hard all summer, tears down and rebuilds the Harley all winter. He is slight in stature, hawk-like in appearance, with unkempt black hair and a wisp of a beard that refuses to grow; I suppose women might relish the rebel, the rake, but I know of none who have gotten close. In a nutshell, it's always been Shifter against the world. No close friends or family to speak of; an aura of menace clings to him like a desperate lover. There have been a few hangers-on in his life, there to feed off what he represents, but they're comrades in horsepower, not in arms.

When Zeb and I launched the Blues that spring, we sounded out Shifter right away. We both felt that under the reptile skin bunkered a worthy guy who'd barely seen the light of day. I still remember the startled look he gave us when we rode out to his ramshackle place south of town, a look like no one had *ever* asked him to join anything. At first he radiated wary incomprehension, then came a moment of unexpected pleasure. He failed to invite us in, but the front door was ajar and I caught a glimpse inside that surprised me: a cozy room lined with filled bookshelves. I thought, *there's a cool guy buried out here, buried deep.*

"Bullshit, Shifter," Zeb voiced in disgust. "Alex and I started the Dry Dogs, and the first thing he said to me was,

'How about we recruit some biker babes for this outfit.' He may have been half-joking, but only half. And no, we ain't the Motorcycle Association nor the Harley Group, but we sure as hell ain't the Vandals, the Boozefighters, or the Drifters. You ain't got a leg to stand on."

Shifter took another shot. "She's hitched to a cherry topper. He run me in."

Surprising everyone, including herself, prospect Emerson fired back, "Come on, Harlin, you were inebriated and urinating in the street."

Shifter froze. Glanced at Zeb. "Can she do that?"

Zeb laughed. "I don't believe there's anything in our so-called bylaws that says the gal can't put up a defense."

"On the plus-side, Harlin," Spoon added, "I'd say it takes courage to hang that thing out in public."

Despite the derisive laughter, Shifter continued to grind. "Her ringman's the law that's always hassling us. We plan a run; coppers'd be laying in wait. Hell, letting Emerson in the Blues'd be like sleeping with the enemy."

I tossed my arms in the air. "Sweet choice of words, Shifter. And man oh man, you'd find conspiracy sproutin' in a peapod. Someone call Oliver North, film at eleven."

"Ahhh...I believe you mean Oliver Stone, the movie director,"

"Yeah, right, Spoony," I muttered disgustedly, "*whomever.*"

Even I couldn't help but add to the laughter that swept the room.

Zeb slammed the table a few times, shouting, "Enough. Stay serious." He sat ramrod straight. "I'm at a loss, Shifter. You believe Robin's here joining up as a spy? You honestly think this ragtag bunch is worth infiltrating? Shit, all we do is drink beer, scrape our knuckles raw wrenching on the bikes here in Hamilton's god-awful dim lit shop, and yell at one another."

Our prez waved off Shifter's attempted rebuttal. Looking squarely at Robin, he reflected a moment, then began. "Now, Ms. Emerson, I'm not backing Harlin's argument, but in a way he has a point. If I were in your shoes, saddling up with these pirates would be my least likely desire. Robin, before we vote, I think it's only natural to ask why you're here tonight."

She had on faded blue jeans, a black pocket tee, and despite the warm evening, wore a dark brown, short-cut leather biker jacket. Light brown hair cascaded over and under the coat's high collar. Robin was collectively striking. Narrow face. Long straight nose. Greco-Roman features that flashed a cover-model look. I noticed that Harlin, throughout his rant, never allowed himself to confront her eye to eye. Shame, what he was missing. The cooling fans in the shop seemed to hum louder as we quit bickering, relaxed, and awaited her reply.

Robin knew it would come down to this. The eternal *why*. She told herself to be honest. Glancing at Harlin Shifter and Gordon Estey sitting across from her and taking a deep breath, she said, "First off, I'm not a secret agent for the sheriff's office." She paused. She wanted to get this right. "My dad taught me to ride out at the farm, mostly lightweight trail bikes. Mom never approved. Two wheels became our little secret. We had a great time. Then life itself intruded. Dad passed on. Schoolin' came on strong, then Wayne and starting a family. On a crazy whim one year back, I took a chunk of the small trust Dad left me and bought the Sportster. Silly, I guess. Felt like Dad was up above smiling though. Wayne was furious; thought it was a waste of money and dangerous to boot. *Sooo...* here I am, acting like a teenager sneaking out of the house. Wayne's unaware I'm here tonight." Shaking her head, she snorted a half-laugh. "Look, I've been blessed with my kids, a husband, and my home. The Harley's apart from all that. I explained to Wayne, this is *my* thing. I'm not running. I need a release; my own time." She looked questionably at all of us. "Any of this making sense?"

The few nods seemed only to add to the stony silence. Robin barely took notice.

"One more thought and then I'll shut up. When I can, when there's time, I'm out riding, but always solo. The bike's a dream. Around Sugar, there are no gals with my itch. To ride with other bikers, share times, learn basic maintenance and stuff; that's my desire. That's why I want to join the Dry Dog Blues, and...I guess that's all I got."

"All right. Ms. Emerson has made her case. There's no need to wait on Ribbs. Let's do this. Robin, you can stay or leave."

"I'll stay."

Zeb provided a look of encouragement. "Gents, the vote is *in* or *out.* Two *outs* denies the nomination. We'll go clockwise around the table. I'll start. "*In.*"

Spoony was next. "A big *in*," he entreated.

I followed. "*In*."

Shifter awaited, arms folded tight across his rawhide vest, his face a mask of indifference. "*Out*."

That left Estey, Shifter's henchman. Noted fact: Gordon Estey has this maddening way about him. He can be easily manipulated. His stance on anything often depends on the last person to twist his arm or pat him encouragingly on the back. Indeed, Estey *was* a weapon in Shifter's arsenal, but there were times "loose cannon" might be an apt depiction. The big guy hesitated. Shifter felt the breeze of uncertainty and turned toward him with a scowl. Robin caught Gordon with a penetrating look. From across the table, she cocked her head and batted big brown eyes, asking for a chance. It was enough. "Aww Harlin, I can't do this. Let's just let her in."

Zeb didn't waste a second. *Wham!* He pounded the table, shouting, "Tally's 4 to 1 for the candidate."

Shifter was struck dumb. Like a cornered diamondback, he leapt onto his betrayer. Knocked over backward on his chair, Estey defended as best he could as Harlin rained down blows. Took Zeb and me all our strength to tear them apart.

Olin Spoon calmly leaned in close to a startled Robin. He winked and whispered, "God, I love this club."

Amidst the melee no one heard Ribbs ride in and enter the shop.

William "Freewheelin'" Ribbs's arrival helped settle everyone down. Observing the four of us untangle, he let out a hoot, "Looks like a typical, harmonious Dry Dog Blues congregation in full swing."

Estey's vote cost him a bloody lip. Our esteemed President Story had caught a flying elbow. A shiner was on its way. Club disagreements turning hostile were nothing new to Ribbs, who stood amused. "Did I miss the Square Dance? Someone forget to promenade?"

How Ribbs felt about Robin Emerson becoming a Dry Dog Blue was anyone's guess. After the tumult, my workshop took on an eerie quiet as Zeb explained that the voice vote stood at 4 to 1 in favor; that Will had the deciding ballot. Stashing his leather, he grasped hand-on-wrist behind his back; then with furrowed brow, he began slowly pacing around our table.

A wiry bantamweight past fifty, Ribbs had always been a man of few words. When we first met, garnering a nonmumbling, complete sentence from him was near impossible. On occasion he would reply muttering in Dylanesque. Ribbs knew Bob Dylan's music. When Harlin and Zeb got him hooked up with the Blues, tagging him with the moniker Freewheelin' from a 60s Dylan LP was a natural.

Will has stood fast here in Sugar City for a decade. His past is sketchy. He'd been a medic in Nam with the 4th Infantry outside Pleiku. An acne-faced teen, he'd survived a deadly firefight during the 1970 Cambodian incursion. Every medic was hit trying to reach wounded GIs pinned down in the crossfire. Ribbs was the only corpsman not dusted off in a body bag. Nothing in his life was ever the same. Returning stateside led to lost years in Mexico. Recrossing the border, always a biker, he hooked up awhile with the outlaw scene in Texas. There had been a marriage somewhere in the 80s. Another restless farewell led him by chance to southeast Iowa. Stopping for coffee in Sugar City, he read that the local nursing home needed help. Now he runs the place.

A favorite story about Ribbs's years at the care center, a tale that pigeonholes him better than any other, concerns the ferrets. By the late 90s, Willie had taken over administration at the manor, including supervising funding operations.

While visiting a girlfriend who worked at the animal shelter, Ribbs was astonished to find two caged ferrets. He had never seen such creatures before and stood fascinated.

He later told me, "Crowded together in that small cage, there wasn't much sparkle in their eyes, and truth be told, the folks at the manor were far from festive. I decided right away, Alex, what the hell, let's see what happens when we put two and two together."

Appropriating $200, Ribbs bought the cage and both homeless inhabitants. On the balance sheets, the purchase was columned under Raising Patient Morale. He was always combating complacency and despair among his charge.

If Ribbs had been aspiring for a spark to liven up the nursing home, he got more than he bargained for. A few residents took to the furry new arrivals right away naming them Red and Ashly for the tint on their silky coats. Those residents were not the only ones aglow. The ferrets were astonished at their newfound freedom. Prairie Manor, with all its facilities, its nooks and crannies, was Ferret Heaven. Ribbs had brought them over in the early evening. Cavorting about had them scampering in every direction. By the time the TV began broadcasting the late news, the rascals were lost, hidden away, sleeping who-knew-where. Will was left scratching his head with an empty cage, thinking, Maybe this wasn't going to work as hoped.

The following day proved classic as early morning work-shifts changed over, and unsuspecting nurses, aides, and administrators arrived for the day. Residents heard the first scream at a few minutes past seven. Nurse Charlene opened a bedpan drawer, and up popped sleepy eyed Ashly. With Charlene racing and shrieking down the tiled hallway (It took all of Ribbs's charm to keep her from quitting on the spot), patients up-and-about shuffled their way to the storage room; delighted to have found one of their weasels.

But where was Red? By mid-afternoon, the big, lazy, crimson-furred male had not yet been located. Had he escaped outside? Ribbs and two volunteer residents walked the surrounding property to no avail.

Confounding the situation, Tim O'Malley from the Iowa Senior Health Regulatory Commission arrived as part of a follow-up state inspection. Ribbs thought, When it rains, it pours.

While the search for Red continued, quite a few residents took time to sit and listen to Wanda Derry play the Knabe grand in the reception hall. Wanda sang and tickled the ivories each Wednesday; mostly hymns and old time favorites. She drew a good crowd.

As Ribbs tells it, Wanda was reverently rendering the gospel hymn *Are Ye Able, Said the Master* when the lost slacker awoke from inside the piano and commenced to slither across the soundboard and cast-iron plate. Arriving behind the music desk, Red reared up on his hind legs, got a firm front paw grip and hoisted himself up.

Wanda's soprano was soaring into the refrain "Thy guiding ra-diance a-bove us" as Red's fuzzy face suddenly appeared atop the sheet music.

Wanda let out a cry heard half a block away. Resident Theodore Hay sitting in the front row reverently ventured she may have hit an operatic high F.

Frightened, Red lost his balance and toppled backward down onto the strings. Wanda had her foot depressing the sustain pedal; thus the ferret's fall created a cacophonous clamor. The resulting ensemble glissando brought the house down.

While Wanda massaged her frightened heart, the audience rushed the piano, grateful for locating the rascal.

Ribbs's inspiration was doomed from the get-go. As the state inspector pointed out, having ferrets running amok was an unprecedented violation of the Iowa Health Code. Like Ribbs, he could clearly see the interest and joy they might provide, but another game plan was needed.

The word was put out as gently as possible. The ferrets had to go. Residents and staff held a meeting to tackle the problem. There weren't enough chairs to accommodate all who attended.

Will knew right then he was onto something. He agreed to take Slacker Red. That drew applause. The lay-about managed to find a new sleeping/hiding spot every day and had become the manor favorite. A mighty cheer arose as Charleen offered her home to sweet Ashly.

Ribbs was amazed at the change the ferrets had wrought. A positive vibe seemed to dilute clusters of sullenness. He followed up. Thursdays became show-and-tell pet visitation day. Animals didn't solve all the problems. Becoming old and feeble creates more potholes than fill; but they give as good a-shot-in-the-arm as any clinic has to offer.

Robin Emerson wouldn't look up (and appeared to be holding her breath) as William Ribbs circled the table. She slouched low as he stopped behind her chair. Her eyes squinted shut waiting for the anvil to fall. Will slowly bent over and whispered in her ear, loud enough for everyone to hear:

"What's a sweetheart like you doin' in a club like this."

She raised her arms, slapped her hands together and gave a whoop. Shifter had a look of disgust and slam-punched Estey in the shoulder. The rest of us exhaled and grinned. Our biker babe was in.

"Someone grab some beers and toss 'em around. We need to toast our newest Dog."

Shifter spoke bluntly, "Believe I'll pass."

Zeb let it go. You picked your battles with Rat Tail. Now was not the time. "What's on tap? We need time tonight to check out Shifter's Shovel. It's been buggin' out on him. Maybe a hot wire."

I have my own agenda tonight, but it's fraught with stage fright. With cans popping open, I'm thinking, *Go for it, it's now or never.* "Zeb, before we get to tackling electrics, I've got something for the club...a proposition."

"Why are my feet screaming, *run!* Run away as fast as you can!"

"Hang on, Spoony, this won't take long. Rumor has it that Lonnie Shimmer's boys are set to cut a wide swath through Wildnut Park to provide Heartland Iron a new access to Highway 12. Takin' some folks by surprise, including me."

I eyed faces of masked indifference. Then, Shifter spoke up. "Didn't we have a run-in with Heartland in the park last summer? We were resting a spell, having a couple beers. They called it private property. Told us to get out."

Zeb nodded, recalling, "Riding back from the party at Conesville. You winged a Busch Light at one of them. They called the cops."

"Did I hit anybody?"

"Missed."

"Damn."

We leather pirates laughed. Robin rolled her eyes.

"Who's the source, Hamilton?" Zeb asked.

I felt fortunate I'd gotten even this far. "The kid told me. Maddy Weber. She drops by the shop now and then hoping to find Jule. I keep teasing the girl I'm building her a chopper. Anyway, her dad's a pencil pusher out at Heartland. He believes the new roadway is a poorly planned, quick-fix joke. No need to destroy the park."

"What are you suggesting, Alex?" Spoon asked.

"Shimmer's set to tear into the place come Friday morning. I'm proposing we back the Weber kid and stop the cut."

"Simple as that," quipped Spoon.

"Simple as that, Olin," I shot back, getting defensive already.

"Hardly our call," Zeb said matter-of-factly.

Shifter turned surly. "How's this gonna shake out, Hamilton? We ride in like the long-lost cavalry? Big face-off: Harleys versus chainsaws? Total blood bath?"

I'd put a bee in their helmets. "Yeah, that's pretty much it, Harlin," I said, doing my damnedest to match his sarcasm.

Robin joined in. "I knew Margo Zaro. She was a close friend. You guys remember her? She taught and coached basketball at the high school, the team that went to State. Died a couple years back from cancer. She would relate stories about Maddy Weber, her team manager, who was probably ten or eleven years old back then. Girl was clever and had pluck. If this Maddy is buckin' for help there's maybe more here than meets the eye. Either way, knowing how Margo was drawn to this girl, her side might be a good one to be on."

"Question is: do we want to be on anyone's side?"

We all sat and mulled Zeb's query for a few moments. Estey tilted toward Shifter. "Didn't you tell me you once hooked up with that gal out at Wildnut years ago? What was her name? Roxy something?"

If Shifter had been cradling a shotgun, he'd have peppered Estey full of holes. Too late, the damage was done.

Ribbs quipped, laughing, "Roxanne Vose? She was a bit long in the tooth, even for you, Harlin."

Estey became mortified, knowing right then he should have let sleeping dogs lie. Shifter was furious. Roxanne was an episode long-buried and meant to stay that way. He was enduring a tough night. The rest of us were in stitches.

Divorcee Roxanne was long gone, but not before her man-eating ways had bedeviled a few strays in Sugar City. But Ms Vose and Harlin? This was new—but the joking banter had gotten us off track. I strove to refocus. "Roll straight guys, stay with me on this. Look, Heartland obviously wants their decision to strip mine Wildnut to fly under the radar. Weber said she's not sure who else knows about the park plan or who even cares. To Shimmer's outfit, it's just a job. Hell, I'm not sure that Heartland even owns the park. But that's not the damn point." I sat up and spoke louder. I wanted to sell this. "Maybe Gordon hit upon something here. Sorry, Harlin." I couldn't help but crack a smile his direction.

He responded closed mouthed with a clenched fist pointed my way.

I kept on. "No one goes to Wildnut anymore, but we all used to. I remember high school. Damn, me and Ann Marie Gilchrist went skinny dippin' out there in the Horn one summer's night, and I don't even want to repeat the stories I've heard of Robin's escapades under the oaks when she was teen cool."

Robin feigned mock astonishment, exclaiming, "Lies, sir! All lies!"

"You are turning a bit scarlet, Ms. Emerson," Zeb chuckled.

I definitely liked this gal. "Just joking, Robin...I think." I stood. "Bottom line, once Heartland built the plant, they pretty much closed the park. The town buried any citizen complaints in a file labeled *Economic Necessity*. Now they want to destroy it. The sawdust is going to fly the day after tomorrow. They got no right. Someone needs to step up. Why not the Dry Dog Blues?" I sat, relieved. I'd given it a good shot.

"Why not call over to county conservation?" Ribbs offered. "Haven't they got a district forester guy? Let them handle it."

Shifter was quick to add, "We go sticking our nose in this, it'll probably wind up costing us a barrel of greenbacks. Last I heard, this outfit couldn't stand for a case of beer. I risk my neck out there, end up arrested...lawyer jack...court costs... who's covering this shit, Hamilton?"

Zeb wanted more. "Sounds like you got a personal stake in this, Alex."

I'd hoped to avoid *that* road. Was I so transparent? I swear, Zeb Story could see through an iron mask, and—I was losing them. "Okay, okay, points well-taken. Considering the natural resource reps; we don't have a lot of time. And Harlin's right, this could prove risky right where it hurts." I glanced at Story. "And dammit, I'll come clean. There is a small stake. The Weber kid drops by the shop out of natural curiosity. Maybe she's got a motorcycle itch. Anybody here recognize that? One time she catches me and Jule smooching in the back room. The two of them start chatting and hit it off. Girlfriend-connection thing. Whatever. The deal is, I've gained a few points with Ms. Spinnetti because I make time for Maddy. So, when the kid shows up to talk oak trees, I listen."

"So we're saving the trees to boost your love life?" Robin grinned.

"Did I really just vote you into this club, Emerson?" My proposition was spinning out of control.

Didn't help when Spoon buried me. "Robin, you have to understand. Mr. Hamilton's love life is like the Cubs winning the World Series. Lots of talk come early spring, but not a whole lot of action by October."

Ah yes, the girlfriend. Juliet Spinnetti's in her final year at Drake Law. The university occupies a shady spot within the city of Des Moines, ninety one point four miles from Sugar. If I could find a shorter route, I'd take it. We met by chance two years back. I was beginning a cross-country solo scoot and Jule was out hitching hoping to catch a ride to a local bus station. We joined forces (long story—*my fault*) and rode one thousand miles two-up on my 88 Harley Softail to her home in Pennsylvania. How looney-tunes was that ride? Let me count the ways. She'd been reported AWOL by frantic parents (*her fault*). Then there was our indecent exposure arrest at a county reservoir (okay—*my fault*). And because every story needs a smash ending, I vividly recall the police escort, the set-to-kill father, and a second arrest (me) at journey's end (a still hotly contested—*her fault*).

I've got eight years on Jule. There have been times though when I've sensed the need to grow and catch up to her. I don't rightly know what our future holds. We're close, but I'm aware her feelings toward me run the gamut. She's the pride of a large Italian clan back East. Juliet Spinnetti mesmerizes with olive skin, full moon eyes, and a soulful look that make my toes dance. She was love at first sight. Can't deny it. Won't.

Amidst the juvenile ribbing, I about gave up. "Hey! I'm being honest here. My link with Jule is going to flip-flop regardless of this Wildnut Park assault. Hear me out. We show up and confront Shimmer's crew. Say they have to move through us to take the trees. We start running over people if we have to. I seriously doubt that'll happen…be a standoff in all likelihood. We hold 'em at bay this Friday. Give folks in town the weekend to latch on to what's happening."

I made a final overture to our president who had been strangely quiet thus far. Without his support, my scheme wasn't going to fly.

"Zeb, when we started the Dogs, I never expected us to become Robin Hood and his band of merry men. Truth is, I didn't know what direction the club might take. But I think we were both after something more than tallying up beers and charging batteries. The Weber kid's got a good cause. Let's help."

Robin Emerson sat back, taking stock. Joining the Blues had been awkward, chancy and hard won. She didn't know any of them well and half-expected a caveman attitude that would quickly drive her up the wall and out. What was transpiring tonight was surprising. There was a respect, albeit grudgingly at times, an admiration for one another here. They might stand toe-to-toe, but the infighting was more good-natured than mean-spirited. Waxing nostalgic, she imagined her dad would have fit right in with this menagerie. The light-hearted laughter that filled the shop at times gave her hope that she might find acceptance here. She turned now with all the others to Zeb Story.

"If the club says no, what are you going to do, Alex?"

"I realize this sounds sorry-assed, but I'll ride out to the park Friday morning and watch the trees come down."

Zeb nodded, remained lost in thought for a spell, then said, "There are a boatload of reasons to shy away from Alexander's proposal. Shifter's spot-on. Someone gets hurt... Heartland Industries and the sheriff both find cause...liability gets tossed around...suddenly we got ourselves both a judicial and financial migraine...and I'm damned certain no one sitting here has got a legal eagle on speed dial. Shimmer will be out there at dawn with all his boys and heavy equipment. He's going to be very unhappy at being turned away. Did I say unhappy? How about ape-shit. They will force the issue. You have to think the confrontation through in those terms, Hamilton. The jacks will outnumber us. Despite our owning the element of surprise, chances are...we do not win this fight. Another consideration, if push comes to shove, we could lose our rides. Any scooter tangling with a bulldozer is coming back to this shop or Spoony's garage in a box. Ribbs, Estey, all of you...think. Is this worth wrecking your bike?" Zeb stared directly at me. "You call for this club to back you, but you ain't got a plan, Straydog."

My heart sank. He was right. I could not counter his fault finding. The whole enchilada was flawed. But surprise, he wasn't through.

"On the flipside, our Founding Father's call to arms has one merit." Zeb paused, leaned back in his chair, and sighed. "It's the right thing to do."

I, Alexander Straydog Hamilton, gasped in amazement.

William Freewheelin Ribbs began drumming the table with both hands.

Olin Spoon joined the percussion.

Gordon Dimmer Estey and Robin Emerson smiled.

Harlin Rat Tail Shifter was incredulous. "Zeb, you can't be serious?"

"I am," Zeb said. "I'm just a washed-out sailor from the west coast, but Sugar City is your home, Harlin. Think it over. If we do nothing, the park's gone. What next? No funds for the library? Who really needs it. It's gone. Dump the school, too. Not enough kids. Hell, busing them on over to the county seat'd be more cost effective. Where do you reckon it all ends."

Zeb waited.

Shifter stayed defiant. "I ain't my brother's keeper."

Our president threw his weight forward. His tilted metal fold-up's wobbly front legs struck the concrete floor with an emphatic screech. "But you *are*," he charged. "Once in a great while, you are."

"No sir, can't do that," Gordon Estey said.

Zeb eyed another dissenter. "Can't do what?"

"Can't say *reckon*."

"Why not?"

"Because, Mr. Story, you're from San Diego. Less than two years you've been here. Californians can't say *reckon*. That's heistin' the vernacular."

Zeb stared at Gordon, perplexed. "When do you think I'll become a prairie-man, Mr. Estey?"

"Clocks move a bit slower here in the Midwest, Mr. Story. Your time will come."

Zeb sat back, hands entwined behind his neck. "I guess you're right."

Gordon leaned toward him. "I reckon I am."

Laughter rocked the room. Even Shifter, shaking his bowed head side to side, looked amused. It was one of those moments one's glad for the company they keep. No one climbs the pedestal to wax philosophic for too long, not in this motorcycle club.

Zeb, laughing the loudest, collected himself. "We'll take a vote. If we agree that Hamilton's scheme is a go, we meet here at dawn on Friday. We ride out together. Olin, you are the home-base-liaison-reserve. We'll need someone to call if we all end up in the county clink."

Spoon looked disappointed. "Alas, my last chance for glory."

Shifter grunted at him. "You'll be thanking your lucky stars for years to come."

Zeb remained focused. "Hard to say if this fight goes down like Ali-Liston or if we're in for a fifteen-rounder. Either way we'll need supplies. Everyone hauls water. God damn, it's turned hot. What is it with Iowa this spring? Ribbs, you're the quartermaster. Whatever you think best and that includes medical. And Robin, you are a member with all rights and privileges, but Wildnut is no cause for you to take on. We've no right to ask you to team up so soon. Might prove to be an ugly spectacle while muddying your boots with this troop."

Shifter dug in his spurs. "Not to mention a possible conflict of interest with Deputy Wayne at the homestead. Nothing we plan here leaves here, eh Emerson?"

Robin met his baiting with resolve. Staring hard, compelling him to look her way, she asked from the corner of her mouth, "Do I get a vote?"

"Yes, ma'am."

"Okay then, we agree to go," she was still eying Shifter, "I'm part of the team."

Zeb ended the wrangle. He wanted to move on. "So be it...your call, Robin. One more matter. A big one. If it's a go, Hamilton will be the field general. This is your show, Straydog. I'm dead serious." He extended me a locked-and-loaded look. "We roll, you lead. You decide the course of action. Rest of us are nothing but cannon fodder."

I felt a chill.

Ribbs half-shouted, "I move we accept the Hamilton proposition by acclamation."

Zeb rapped his remaining twig of a gavel on the table a few times and called for a vote. "All for the Wildnut Park rescue say *aye*."

"*Ayes*" rang out.

"Opposed?"

Silence.

I sat stunned. What had I done?

Zeb said, "Any last words, Commander Hamilton?"

My reply was immediate, from out of nowhere. "Spartans at Thermopylae."

Shifter snapped, "They were slaughtered!"

I leaned toward him with a half-crazed grin, whispering, "Ahhh, but their legend lives, Mr. Shifter. The legend lives on."

6
THE LAW STUDENT

Why, at times, do we plunge ahead, so cocksure we're right, so confident in our quest? Then, sha-boom! We're ambushed by second thoughts and a huge loss of nerve. I had set wheels in motion with both the Weber kid and the Blues. Problem being (along with my cold feet), I had a half-hatched plan I'd divulged to no one. I hadn't been completely open or honest with either party.

Why was I packing this nine-hundred-pound gorilla on my shoulders? Oak trees? Was Paul Bunyan a distant relative? What was so empty in my life that I would jump at the chance to play hero to a fourteen-year-old girl? And why harbor a secret scheme that might put her in harm's way? I needed to call the whole confrontation off. Instead, like an AA member reaching for 101-proof Wild Turkey, I opened yet another door inviting in lunacy and dialed up Juliet Spinnetti.

"Drake Law cram room, bring it."

"Why doesn't Jule ever answer the phone?"

"Ah, let me guess. The founding-father biker dude stalking my roomie."

"Get over yourself, Marsha. Holler for Jule."

Marsha Sticker, Jule's classmate and roommate, was always a handful; the thorny black rose, always on guard, blocking my advance.

"I'm at a loss Hamilton. She's young, smart, vivacious... building toward a brilliant law career, and yet there's this hiccup, this flaw: you. What in sweet justice does she see in you?"

With Sticker, I learned early on to keep slinging. "We're soul mates, and by the way, the two of us are eloping tonight. I'm calling to synchronize our Rolexes...to double check the window's unlatched and she's got the bed sheets tied together good and tight. Damn it Sticker, put her on the line!"

I heard a belch. "I come with the prenuptial, Hamilton. Con my girl into your heathen leather circle and I'll be oiling up the dueling pistol."

"*Get a life!!*" I raged, exasperated.

"Hi, sweetie. I got a life. Law student...wild party animal... remember?"

"Hey, you. Sorry. Easier dealing with the Spanish Inquisition than your psycho roommate. Man, that gal is a wasp up my pant leg."

Jule laughed that wonderful sound. "She watches over me, Alex. That's a good thing, no? Besides, it's not you. If Prince William was at my doorstep she'd react the same. Actually, I think she likes you. In her own words: 'At least he's not some boring litigator.'"

"Yeah, right."

"Enough of my sidekick. To what do I owe the pleasure?"

"First off, there's news from the Sugar City front. Ms. Robin Emerson is now a full-fledged Dry Dog Blue."

"No way! How cool. How'd she cruise past Harlin?"

"Let's just call it a bumpy ride. Next, and most importantly, I miss you, Juliet. I miss us...the kissing part. I'm a million behind."

Oftentimes I felt the two of us were like bumper cars, racing around and around, randomly ricocheting off sideboards, once in a great while crashing into one another. We had a pact to stay at loose ends as she grinded forward to a degree in law and the inevitable bout with the bar exam. The last circumstance she needed was her mind drifting over a dubious love affair. She wasn't convinced she was in love. I knew that. We'd had one crazy motorcycle ride together, and how easy it was to conjure up that last night on the road. Riding eastward at dusk, I'd asked, "Stars or bulbs?" That magic night. The crammed tent. Kissing. Giggling. Fumbling about in the dark. Light rain falling. The warmth. My god, you can build a lifetime of commitment around such a night. Can't you? To Jules, the journey was a one-shot, chancy, way-out-of-character adventure. But I was lassoed. Somewhere between Iowa and Pennsylvania I lost my heart to her, and I didn't want it back.

"A million behind. Hmmm, listen Hamilton, don't stop counting. Hey! Before I forget. When we're together next, I've a favor to ask."

"Actually, me too. Let's do them now. You first."

"All right. I've been riding. I know, I know, *carefully* riding, that old Honda you found for me. Doing quite well, thank you very much. Here's the deal: I'm charged to move on up, Straydog. I'm asking you to let me ride solo on your Harley. Someplace super safe. How about it?"

"The Softail's a lot of bike, Jule."

"I'm ready."

"Anything goes wrong, you fall, get hurt, your dad would personally Zippo my funeral pyre."

"I'll be fine. Maybe cozy around some vacant parking lot. Come on, Bike Boy, I want to feel that throbbing power between my legs."

"Wouldn't I do instead?"

"Smart guy. Think about it, okay? Now, what's your favor?"

I shored up my courage and got right to the point. "I need info...legal type."

Jule let out a leery, "Right up my alley. Something happen?"

"Nothing yet. I'm curious about kidnapping. I mean, is it a federal law, or do individual states have their own rules? And if Iowa has an abduction thing on the books, how is it defined?"

The line went dead for a spell.

"You're scaring me here, lover."

"Sorry. To be honest, Jule, I'd rather back off on the specifics. I'm asking you to review the State regs, if there are any, and explain them to me in layman's terms. That's the favor. And I know this is last minute, but I need an answer by tomorrow night."

"Why the rush?"

"Ummm, plans are in place. Things are coming to a head."

"Kidnapping? Plans? Vague things?" Jule's voice vented agitation. "Is this a Sugar City problem? I don't need to review squat. Yes, Iowa does have its very own body snatch precept, and it covers more than: Yo, I've got your kid. Pay the ransom."

"Such as?"

"Basically, Alex, if the State can substantiate you've abducted someone and have assumed custody and control, you will be charged under the kidnapping statute. Need I remind you, sir, penalties are severe."

I sensed her bewilderment but pushed on. "Within Iowa, could the Feds become involved?"

"Absolutely. No border crossing required. If the state attorney and law enforcement feel the need for federal cavalry, the bugles will blow. Give, Hamilton. What in the world is going on?"

No way was I going to involve her in Wildnut Park. "Look, Jule. I made a vow early on that no matter how long the two of us lasted, five days or five decades, that I'd never lie to you about anything. But right now I'm staying mum. Just...trust me. Okay?"

"No, I'm not trusting anything here. Thank you for your vow, but withholding is a type of lying."

"How's about we get together Saturday night? I'll drive up."

"What, now you're changing the subject?"

"Give me one more day on this. I'll fill in the blanks. I promise. I'm overstating the case. Not to worry."

"Favor for a favor, Mr. Hamilton. I'm not worried. I'm totally lost at my end. Don't go tractor-jacking the farmer's daughter. Might put a kink in our relationship."

"Agreed, Ms. Spinnetti...favor for a favor."

"Gotta run, Alex. Late for a night class. Kisses."

She was gone. I felt a little woozy, and why not. It had been bonkers all day. I had tomorrow to think this through—maybe touch base with Madison Weber—level more with Zeb—lay the scheme all out to Jule. Charged with kidnapping? Shitsville! Was that possible? Decision time, and my gut was churning and turning into knots. Some field general.

THURSDAY, MAY 10, 2001

Worried Midwest forecasters are closely monitoring two fronts, fearing the impact from a late last gasp of winter versus an early blast of summer heat.

Alarmed by the vast temperature contrast between two weather systems rapidly approaching one another from the northwest and south, respectively, the National Weather Service has issued a tornado watch for eastern Kansas and northern Missouri.

The Storm Prediction Center in Norman, Oklahoma has also issued a severe thunderstorm watch for extreme southeastern Nebraska and all of southern Iowa.

Alerts will remain in effect throughout today, May 10, until noon, May 11.

7
THE NEWS CREW

"Good morning, KBOX News Channel 6. This is Gina."

Madison Weber strived to lower her voice. "I'd like to speak to an investigative reporter."

Amused at the masked intonation, Gina hollered into the busy newsroom, "Do we have an investigative reporter in the house?"

Madison heard a lot of laughter coming through the line. Finally: "Joan Chase here, and you are?"

She went as low as she dared. "The Voice of Reason."

"Uh huh. First question, Ms. Reason: how old are you?"

"Eighteen."

"Alright, age eighteen, give or take a few years. Why the call?"

"I need your help to stop a crime."

"What kind of crime?"

"A crime against nature."

Joan sighed. "Give me a few specifics, Reason."

"Right. At Wildnut Park, outside Sugar City. They are going to cut down our trees."

"Why?"

"To build a stupid road. You have to get the story on the TV news tonight to stop them."

Joan was aware of the caller's rising desperation as well as a return to her normal voice, noticeably higher now than at the start of their conversation. She was willing to play along. "Who's 'them'?"

"Heartland Ironworks, and they're starting tomorrow morning so you have to hurry."

"Look, honey, I'm not sure how this Des Moines station can help you. Sugar City is near the edge of our broadcast DMA. Maybe beyond. How about trying someone local?"

"But you have to help. My friends and I will be at the park protesting. No one knows the oaks are going to be destroyed. You can change that."

"Can I have your real name, Reason? A number where the station can reach you?"

"Just do what you can. *Please!*" Madison hung up.

KBOX News Director George Ridgefield had been half-listening and noticed Joan hanging onto a dead line. "What was that all about?"

"That," said Joan, "was the Voice of Reason, in her early teens, near tears, trying to save trees at a place called Wildnut Park." She shrugged, dispirited. "Another development or some such. Another, and I quote, 'crime against nature.'"

George failed to detect her drift. "Why's our station the recipient of every bleeding-heart crackpot in Iowa?"

Joan frowned. "You know, George, there was a time we rushed into journalism to make our world a better place."

"Let's not get started, Joan."

She wasn't listening. She called out, "Gina, do we still have that cub reporter on staff? The kid from Drake?"

Gina shouted, "She'll be in this afternoon. Kelly Bauer."

George Ridgefield grew attentive. "For heaven's sake, Joan, what are you thinking? We've hardly time for this nonsense."

Joan gave him an indignant smile. "I'll have Kelly make a few calls. What could it hurt?"

8
THE BLUES

Robin saw him first, up ahead, the motorcycle parked by the roadside, leaning on its kickstand. They were two miles from town. She, Wayne, and the kids were returning mid-morning from the county courthouse after seeking answers to why their property taxes had risen 60 percent. They'd had no new additions. Their old place still harbored the leaky roof and crumbling foundation. The assessor's explanation of higher resale prices and state-mandated increases had left them both ill-tempered.

Didn't help matters when Robin spied Shifter and told her husband to pull over. Wayne recognized the biker, coughed up an indulgent chuckle, and said, "No way, let him push it in."

Robin turned cat-quick to her husband. "Dammit, Wayne, pull over now!" Her tone of voice awoke their two sleepy-eyes buckled up in the back. They heard their mom rail, "Stranded motorist. Law officer charged with aiding the public. Ring a bell, Wayne?"

"Aww, all right, Jesus." Wayne, clearly annoyed, hit the brakes and maneuvered their clunky Dodge Caravan to a stop some thirty yards past the stranded Harley.

Robin peered through the windshield eying an eerie sky of unnatural colors. The humidity outside was wilting any patience she and her husband had left for one another. Not a whiff of a breeze, but clouds were gathering. She sensed a storm poised to strike like a coiled cobra hidden in a closet. With the motor idling, she softened, "Listen, Wayne, I know you and Shifter have had run-ins in the past, so I'll manage this. You stay with the kids. Rain's on the way. If we have to, he can slide in back. We'll drop him off at Hamilton's shop in town. How about it?"

Wayne was incredulous. "What do you mean you'll handle this? Since when do you even know this guy?!"

His question set loose an anxiety attack. She had been waiting for a better time to tell him, but now Shifter's predicament provided an opportune moment if ever there was one. Do it, she scolded herself, do it now! "That broke-down guy behind us is a biker buddy. I joined the Dry Dog Blues yesterday." She snorted a half-remembered laugh. "They actually voted me in. I believe there's an unwritten rule that states you don't leave a club bro stranded out in the middle of nowhere."

Wayne sat in disbelief. "Have you gone completely nuts?"

She hardly heard him. "Just...just stay in the car." She was out the passenger-side door walking in haste toward the cycle.

Tools scattered about on gravel, seat off, kneeling, inspecting battery cables and wiring, Shifter looked pissed. Nearing him, Robin tried to be coy. Keep it light, girl. "Out of gas?"

Shifter ignored her.

Pointing upward at the darkening southwest horizon, Robin said, "Seeing as how that storm's about to dump a tidal wave of rain on your head, I thought maybe you could use a helping hand."

No response.

Facing back to the van, she said, "You should jump in, catch a ride to town."

Nothing.

This guy was so exasperating. "Got a rope? How 'bout a tow in?"

Dead eyed, Shifter growled, "I'd rather drown in the storm."

Robin stood motionless, flabbergasted. She thought, *The hell with this. What an asshole.* Humiliated, she spun about. Halfway back, she slowed her pace and reconsidered. She'd wanted into the Blues. She'd overcome her apprehension and had gone to that meeting. But truly, she was a member in name only. Challenges lay ahead, and Harlin Shifter was certainly one of them. Bottom line, this was not the time to cut-and-run.

Striding quickly to the driver's side, she leaned in and pecked Wayne on the cheek, then confounded him further.

"He's nearly set. Wants a bit of help. I'll stay and ride back with him. You go on ahead with the kids. We'll meet at the Kum and Go. We need to fill up anyway."

Wayne was red-faced furious. "This is insane. Riding with that hoodlum. Storm about to strike any minute." He shook his head. "Get in! We gotta talk. I don't know where you're coming from. I don't know where you're going."

Dead silence ensued. Robin could not for the life of her think of a single thing to say. Time was wasting. She nodded an acceptance. "Later, Wayne." Smiling at her two now wide-eyed worrywarts in the back seat, she reassured them, "See you both in a few minutes." She took one step back, turned, and left.

Wayne threw the van into drive and raced off, spinning the tires, hurling gravel back at his retreating wife. Robin flinched from the sting of small stones ripping into her backside. For an instant she felt like flipping her husband the bird. Let him catch that in the rearview mirror! Wow, their marriage needed work. And the kids tagging along, off from school due to a teachers workshop or somesuch—why today? They had already witnessed too much mom and dad anger. Not good. She all but wilted when rehashing the past shouting spats as she and Wayne sought common ground. She turned, squinting at disappearing taillights. Maybe Wayne was right to question. Where *was* she going? Taking the moment, she closed her eyes and tried to shake herself free—for the wind was picking up and in turning back, the bike was still sitting.

Coming close, Robin saw Shifter sporting a smirk. He cracked, "Trouble in paradise?"

Robin dismissed him. He'd opened up a line of conversation that was completely out of bounds. "My private life is the least of your concerns, Mr. Shifter." Glancing again at the approaching storm caused her to shudder. "We've got to get this piece of Milwaukee iron moving, pronto."

"Doesn't look good."

Robin grew alarmed. "Talk to me, Harlin. What's going on here?"

He ran a hand through his hair, scratching long black curls. "She cut out on me. Been happening at odd times all spring. Something's warming up, getting hot, and shutting her down. Usually wait a spell. She'll cool and refire."

"We can't wait!"

Shifter eyed the sky. "No shit. I've got an open circuit. Somewhere. Somehow." He looked up at her, angry and disgusted. "The Dogs were supposed to help solve this last night. But no, we get so wrapped up trying to figure you out plus Hamilton's crazy scheme, and whatayaknow, there's no time to trouble-shoot the bike and here we freaking sit."

As if on cue, the sky offered up a frightening clap of thunder. Trying hard not to sound frantic, Robin asked, "Why here, why the breakdown at this spot?"

Harlin was indignant. Then, as an afterthought, said, "Hit a pothole back a ways. She died."

Robin edged closer to him. "You say the bike's been cutting out all spring. Think, Harlin...last winter or maybe in March and April, you're working on the bike, right? Rebuilding projects. Any possible connection?"

Shifter's demeanor changed. Squinting at Robin Emerson with interest, recognizing her hindsight, he began taking inventory. An idea took root and grew. "Had the tanks painted. Slaved all winter on the design. HawkArt Hog in Iowa City brushed on the graphics. Sprayed the finishing coats at my place."

Dark clouds were directly overhead. Thunder rumbled. Wind whipped up loose sand. The transformation from day to night was nearly complete. For a moment, the two of them were oblivious to the tempest about to overwhelm them. They were face-to-face; lost in thought. He shouted, "Maybe a winner. You hold. I'll loosen the bolts."

Shifter had a wrench turning in a flash. Robin was on her knees lightly gripping the two gas tanks; silently praying for a minor miracle. She called out, "Ignition on?"

Concentrating feverishly, Harlin checked the switch, affirming, "Yeah, yeah. Shake 'em a bit." As he loosened first the upper then the lower bolts, Robin felt the tanks break free from the bike's frame. Jostling them a bit, the Harley's speedo suddenly lit up. The headlight now beamed into the gathering darkness. Robin shook her head with delight. The only staging missing from this surreal scene were bellowing trumpets.

With gusting wind and rolling thunder, they fought to be heard. She cried out, "The wiring must be pinched!"

Harlin understood. "Metal on metal, babes. There's no time to locate the culprit. We've got to roll. I'll leave them a tad loose. Only chance we got"

Frantically they gathered up tools. He slung a leg over the seat and slammed his boot into the kicker, jamming his foot down hard once, twice, three times: nothing—hardly a sputter. Cursing, he tried a fourth time. *Ka-boom!* The cycle roared to life. Robin relished the sweet sound as the Harley settled into a staccato idle. She vaulted onto the back fender pylon. Harlin engaged the clutch and heel-jammed into first. Robin leaned forward as close as possible, her chest on his backside, reaching around with both arms to grab and steady the vibrating gas tanks. They weren't moving.

Inexplicably, Harlin turned sideways and shouted above mother nature's din and the Harley's throttle. "Ya' know, Emerson, you never said whether you favored my custom paint job."

Completely agitated at the delay, she taunted, "Oh yeah, skulls, dragons, naked babes...hell, Shifter, I'm enchanted."

Lightning streaked across the sky.

She slapped the back of his head and screamed, "Now *go, go, go!*"

They almost made it. The deluge began a half mile from overhead cover. Harlin had to slow to a crawl. In haste, he'd nearly sent the bike hydroplaning into the ditch. Still, even at a snail's pace, control was near impossible in the gale-driven, torrential downpour.

After what felt an eternity, they water-wheeled to town, alert, upright, alive, halting under the gas pump canopy at the convenience store; the two of them, drenched, chilled, and oh so grateful. That the bike was still running was near-scandalous.

Robin awarded Shifter with a light squeeze at the waist. Without a word, she slipped off the bike, walked slowly to the van, and squished into the front seat. Wayne found a towel to dry her face and matted hair. "Jesus, Robin," he implored, "we've got to get home before you catch pneumonia."

"You okay, Mommy?" Liza asked from the back seat.

Robin turned seeing two small, worried faces, "I'm fine, sweethearts," then, chuckled in self-amusement, "I'm just really, *really* soaked."

The rain slackened. Shifter was standing beside his bike. Wayne had the motor running, heater fan on, ready to move—when the hail hit. Golf ball and baseball sized jagged ice drummed down onto the tin metal overhead. The sound was akin to a thousand riveters—percussionist Keith Moon rocking out in full frenzy on Heaven's drum kit. Through the mist and the roar, Harlin and Robin located one another and exchanged a wide-eyed look. They'd been twenty seconds from disaster.

The hail lasted a minute then stopped as suddenly as it began. Cars and pick-ups parked unprotected bore witness to the onslaught of ice. Hoods and tops were badly pockmarked. Windshields cracked. A sun roof had shattered.

Disoriented, Robin mumbled out loud, "Good Lord." Wayne, bowing and shaking his head, had a facial expression that screamed, *I warned you,* but simply said, "We're going home."

Robin had the window open. She was bent over, unlacing her shoes, so the kids were the first to see him striding up to the van. They didn't say a word. Wayne sensed his presence, saw his hands grip the passenger side door, and instinctively kept the Caravan in neutral. Robin was oblivious, facing forward and downward attempting to pull off a stubborn, soaked shoe. Shifter leaned inside, got close, and kissed her on the cheek. Startled, she flinched and turned. Shifter kissed her again, full on the lips, whispering, "Thanks, you saved us."

Robin felt warm blood gush to her cheeks rooting out, for the moment at least, the chill brought on by the wild cycle ride. Wayne shouted angrily, "*Hey* buddy, *back off!*" He was too late. With a quick nod and grin to the kids, Shifter was gone, back on his bike and on down the road. She sat stone still. Wayne was quiet; getting the van moving at last. Liza broke the awkward silence. "Mommy, that man winked at me."

"It's okay, honey, he was just being...", Being what, she mused? The entire episode had been extraordinary. Her mind was full of wonder. Grateful? Nice? Sweet kiss? Harlin Shifter? The kiss—no wait, there were two kisses!

From behind, Robin's nine year old son Michael broke her reverie. "Mom, you're shivering."

"I'm fine, sweetie, just wet and weary." Robin sat erect, breathing deep, then smiled back at the two of them. "I'm okay."

Zeb Story pulled up to the Bradbury place past noon as expected. Just another work order, but instinctively he knew he was tempting fate. An ex-submariner, he coveted the feeling of being in control no matter the situation. Anticipation is crucial, and he'd swear by the ghost of Vice Admiral Rickover that he had a history of being at-the-ready no matter the situation. He knew this to be true. Checking the rear view mirror, he saw himself resourceful and perceptive. Well—maybe on a nuclear powered tin can. Not here. If the truth be told, he was hopelessly lost at what might lay in store. Shaking his head, admonishing himself for sweating palms, Zeb grabbed a tool case and ambled toward the front door. Jessi had it half-open, awaiting him.

Gazing up at the large, elegant, two-story biscuit-box farm house, Zeb's memory took flight, returning to his youth and a young boy's first trip to an amusement park, gaping at the mammoth wooden roller coaster. What was the name? Ah yes, The Black Python. He recalled that ominous click, click, click as the coaster climbed that first pinnacle, his hands holding onto the car rail in a death grip, not sure his eyes would open to witness the summit and the adrenalin-rush, high-speed plunge to follow. He trembled, dispelling the daydream, and greeted his one o'clock; his stomach flip-flopping, just as it did riding the great-snake so many years ago. He whispered to himself: "Oh boy."

Jessi had been a nervous wreck all morning, furious at herself for asking Zeb's daughter Ana to set up this appointment. What had she been thinking? There were other plumbers to call. Idiot. Too late now. Putting on a face, she smiled a hello and got one in return.

"Ms. Bradbury," Zeb gave a mock salute.

"Mr. Story, so glad you're here. Survived the hail stones, I see."

"Made out better than the old Econoline," waving at the service van. "Roof's battered like someone took a ball-peen hammer to it...an improvement, actually. What seems to be the problem here?"

"Drains are super slow. Toilet barely flushes. I mean, the plumbing's old and has never been great..."

Her words were lost to a vision of worn jeans with a faded blue-print flannel shirt, sleeves rolled haphazardly. She appeared harried, but summer fresh and strikingly pretty. Why had he been in such denial over this woman these many months? His heart was flip-flopping, not his stomach. Don't stare, he reprimanded himself. "Point me to the basement. I'll have a look."

"Great. I'm hanging laundry out back. Come find me if I can be of any help."

Didn't take Zeb long to ascertain the problem. The plumbing was ancient but solid. The thin breather pipe that rose through the house and protruded above the roof was likely clogged. There was no back-draft. The system couldn't exhale. Attaching a Drain King to her garden hose, he had Jessi on the roof, forcing water down into the 'breather'—no luck. Returning to the basement, Zeb cut a pipe segment and ran a router on up, penetrating the clog at last. Having climbed down off the roof and now standing alongside, Jessi gave out a yelp, jumping clear. Years of accumulated gunk cascaded onto the basement floor. Zeb sensed the entire pipe network shudder with a sigh of relief.

Afterward they were in the kitchen. Jessi was happily running water through the sink drain. "You're a miracle worker, Story." She smiled at him.

There was no thinking now-or-never and certainly no premeditation. Stuff happens. Human appendages relocate without brain impulses. Zeb took a few steps toward her.

She was still smiling, asking, "What are you doing?"

"Moving closer."

"Why?"

"Can't kiss you from where I'm standing."

"I don't think that's a good idea."

Zeb closed. "Can't start a fire without a spark."

Jessi stood still. "Don't go quoting Springsteen, either."

They were face-to-face, both hesitant. Zeb reached and held her hand. "Okay, say 'no' within three seconds or...we'll chance it."

Jessi closed her eyes, tensing up as if cringing for an electric shock. She got one. Zeb kissed her with passion.

They broke apart. Alarmed over what they'd done, Zeb retreated. He didn't get far. Jessi made a lunge, threw her arms around his neck, and feverishly kissed him back. No one was retreating now. Catching her breath she let her arms drop, slowly caressing him. "Why, Mr. Story, I do believe you're trembling."

Zeb held her close, clasping his hands around her waist. "Stage fright, I reckon," smiling to himself instantly, recalling Gordon Estey's reprimand.

Not letting go, Jessi leaned her head back to study his green-gray eyes and handsome face. "If you're going to seduce me, Zeb Story, you best do it now before I regain my sanity."

Both let go. Neither spoke. They exchanged looks of confusion, a spot of indecision perhaps, before complicating their lives. Then, in a flash, Jessi was lifted off her feet and cradled in his arms. As they passed by the wall clock in the hallway, she made a mental note. It was two p.m. God, I'm in the middle of my own trashy romance novel.

There was unexpected joy in their lovemaking. For Zeb, capsized by a ravaging hunger, the pure physical explosion was over too quickly.

Afterward, lying side by side, gently touching, they quietly talked about their personal lives: the hurt, the loss, the loneliness, and anger. Then, suspending the past and returning, once more, to their perfect summer's *affaire d'amour,* Jessi teasingly chided him over the rock-n-roll quote.

Zeb lay back on the pillow and laughed, "Did I really say that?"

Jessi snuggled and began tracing her fingers down and around this beautiful man. "Maybe because my daughter told you I have a 'thing' for the Boss."

"Actually, no, but I have been informed by a certain thirteen-year-old that you are a hot babe in the shower."

Jessi stopped, astonished. "You jest!"

Zeb grinned, "From the mouths of babes."

"She's in *so* much trouble." Jessi resumed tracing. "Where were we?"

Zeb reached for her. "Still moving closer."

Wondrously fulfilled, they fell back in an afterglow that had been buried for far too long. Jessi pinched herself. Surely I'm daydreaming. But, turning her head, there he was, big as life. Giddy, she said, "Feeling pretty good about yourself, are ya?"

Zeb returned a self-satisfied grin.

Rolling on her hip, perched on an elbow and confronting him, she teased, "This why submariners keep yelling up-scope in the movies?"

He grimaced. "Truth be told, we're usually screaming, dive! *Dive!*"

They both snorted and then belly laughed themselves to tears.

Jess collected herself. "Look at me, Story."

Zeb's eyes poured over her lean naked body.

She playfully punched his arm. "No! I mean my face, Mr. Story. I want your undivided attention. Wait." Sliding from the bed, she went about locating her robe. Zeb followed her every move. Covering herself, she curled back in next to him. "Now concentrate, this is important."

"Shoot."

Jessi knew something needed to be said. "All right, here goes. I'm not a puritan. I'm not a prude. But, I'm a *good* girl, Zeb Story, and I want you to know I've never, I mean *never*, done anything like this in my entire life."

He didn't say a word.

"I'm off the charts here. *You're off the charts, Story!*" Jessi kissed him on the cheek. "I want you out of my bed, dressed, and on your way. No more ravishing the customers." Observing the bedside alarm, she bolted upright. "God, it's a quarter to four. Your Ana is spending the night and both girls will be here any minute."

"What are you going to tell them?"

"Good Lord, nothing."

Zeb studied her. "They both know I planned to be here. They'll see right through you."

Not wanting to stew over any sort of explanation to the kids, she changed the subject. "About the girls...Rachel has been preoccupied the past couple of days. Any strange vibes coming from Ana?"

Zeb thought a moment then shook his head. "Nothing obvious." He rolled from the bed, grabbing clothes. "What do I do an hour from now when I'm overcome with desire to kiss you again?"

She felt herself blushing and thought, *Has anyone ever said such a thing to me?* He had one leg in his pants; the other dangling, as she reached out and gently pushed him off-balance. "Get a move on. Guys dress in, like, what...ten seconds? I need time to fathom this...fathom us. Whatever this is...we are? Oh my, listen to me. I'm a babbling noodlehead. More? Really?"

Zeb finished buttoning his shirt, then reached for her and planted a last lingering kiss. "You're a beautiful noodlehead, Jessica Bradbury. Remember me to my daughter tonight."

Standing by the service van, he turned and waved. Subconsciously he always knew he'd begin again. He hadn't dreamed, though, that the rekindling would be so heartfelt.

Outside the door, Jessi returned his wave, thinking she'd taken complete leave of her senses.

9
THE IRONWORKS

Rita Gunsolley checked the wall clock: 4:25 p.m. She reached for the ringing phone, mumbling, "Five more minutes and I'm heading home." Picking up, she answered, "Heartland Ironworks, how may I direct your call?"

"Kelly Bauer from KBOX News, Des Moines, asking for the plant supervisor."

"That would be Richard Lester, Ms. Bauer. Unfortunately, Mr. Lester is at our corporate headquarters in Chicago until early next week."

Kelly sensed a brush-off. "Is there a plant manager or assistant supervisor available?"

"I'm Rita Gunsolley, Mr. Lester's personal secretary." She was taking a chance here, nearly stumbling over the contrived job label. Hah. Plant gal-Friday was more like it. "Might I ask what this call is in reference to?"

"Sure." Kelly was chewing gum and snapped a bubble. "The station got a call this morning about you folks destroying an old oak grove to build a road. The caller was upset about the tree loss. KBOX is following up and asking for a company statement."

Rita nearly dropped the phone. She recalled Lester's secretive conversations, his cautioning her not to divulge the goings-on with Lonnie Shimmer and others. She'd been angry, wanting to confront him, but in the end lost courage and had done nothing, feeling ashamed. But in a small town, word gets around, and now, like a gift, here were the media, of all people, at her doorstep.

She knew that talking to the likes of Kelly Bauer on her own was probably against company policy, frowned upon at the very least. She might in fact be risking her job. If let go, she would miss it, enjoying the good-natured give-and-take of the workplace. But Lester's arrival had altered the dynamics at Heartland. She had sensed, from muttered conversation around the coffee urn, an undercurrent of resentment building within plant production: cutting corners, a slippage in quality control—now this park thing.

So *do* something, Gunsolley, she challenged herself. Someone out there has backbone. Ms. Bauer's a second chance. Play a role. She tightened her grip on the receiver and said, "I'm fully aware of Heartland's plans for our new access road." Attempting to add a touch of conspiracy to her voice, a tone she hoped the reporter would pick up on, she followed up, "I'm quite capable of supplying your station with background details."

10
AUTUMN

Dorothy Hook shouted upstairs. "Pick up, Autumn. Summer's on the line." Thirty years living in the big, old, rambling Hook farmhouse. Thirty years telling herself to install an intercom. Still waiting.

Autumn found the cordless laying on the bed. "Hey, Hot Stuff, what's cooking up in Pantherland?"

"Just between you and me, Auti, our names are tops, but every time mom yells Autumn and Summer together, it sounds like a seasonal weather report."

Autumn laughed. "Got that right. And what if they had two more kids?"

"Ho boy...they would be Winter and Spring, right?"

"Yeah. What'll we call them? You're Hot Stuff. I'm Cool Down. Guess that makes them...hmm...how about Deep Freeze and Warm Up?"

Summer gave out a whoop, adding, "Perfect. Tell pops to get right on it."

Hearing shrieks of laughter float down the stairwell, Dorothy shook her head wistfully. Remembering how excited and proud they all felt when Summer was awarded the basketball scholarship at the University of Northern Iowa. Now, three years along, despite her daughter's success, she still lamented not having her home on a day-to-day basis. Just the thought of Autumn eventually fleeing the coop gave her a chill. But right this minute, what a good feeling to hear sisterly laughter fill the house. Gracious, what in the world are they going on about?

"Stop, Summer, my stomach hurts. Can we change the subject? This is all too terrifying to contemplate. When ya' coming home? I miss you."

"Finals are next week, then I'm heading down to the farm."

"Goody. So what's happening? Boyfriends? Can you keep fending them off?"

"Yeah, right. Actually, I have met someone."

"*Really!* Details. Details."

"Relax. Nothing earth-shattering, just a guy in chem lab. His name is Dexter Longbridge, and he does come equipped with the two Hook prerequisites, i.e.; he's tall and he breathes."

Autumn sensed her sister turning coy. Maybe this potentially was front-page stuff. "Come on, sis, give a little. How handsome is our Mr. Longbridge? Are you really dating a Dexter?"

"Watch it, Cool Down. I happen to think the name Dexter is kinda trendy. And handsome? Mmmmmmmm...well, he's thin, shy, brainy, and a bit nerdy. Once you get past the glasses and punk hair pointing every which way, I'd say he's sorta cute."

"Bring him home with you. Pops will have him choring in no time. Have you told him he's dating a superstar?"

Summer took a more somber tone. "First off, we're not seriously dating or anything. Don't get carried away, sis. And, so far, I've never mentioned basketball...the team...none of it."

"Why not?"

"Golly, I don't know. Maybe 'cause I'm in uniform 24/7. Practice, practice, study; sleep. Practice, practice, study; sleep. That's my whole boring life. Frankly, sis, I think I was tired of hoops by the tenth grade. I'm twenty and still wallowing in elbows, turnovers, set-shots, and smelly socks. Dexter is new and different...separate from the team. I like that."

"Sounds to me that you like *him*. So go have some fun."

"I told you, I'm at the gym seven days a week. I don't know *fun*, plus, Dexter's a techie lab-rat. I don't think he knows *fun*, either."

"Well find out, Hot Stuff. Go discover it together. You'll be a prairie-land Adam and Eve. Lots of kissing, sex, and stuff."

"Autumn Hook! How old are you?!"

Autumn giggled. "I'm happy for you, sis, and I'm sure next fall you'll, like, totally turn him on with your crossover dribble."

Summer laughed. Attending UNI was cool, but she loved and missed her younger sister. Funny, growing up, how close they'd always been despite being seven years apart. Maybe their age difference was key. Mom would surely disagree, but she didn't remember a serious sister spat. "Hey, speaking about next fall, listen up. Come this September you'll be in high school. Enjoy it, Autumn. Spread your wings. Don't become just a sweaty hoopster like me. Try all kinds of stuff; music, theater, the school paper. Don't pigeonhole yourself, okay? That's it...my older sib lecture of the day."

"Come on, sis, you were a Sugar City legend in your own time."

"Auti! I went to prom with Bobbie Brinkerhoff, remember? The two dateless wonders."

"But you told me you danced with lots of boys there."

"True, but that's not the same as being asked to the prom. I was a too-tall basketball freak who palled around with her teammates. Heck, I wasn't that close to the rest of my classmates. Big mistake. Boys were like the unknown X-factor. Take heed, little sister. But enough of me, what's on in your world; and best watch what you say. Mom's probably right outside your room pretending to sweep the carpet."

"She hates being a spy," Autumn whispered, "but in her own words, The hens will roost over golden eggs before my daughters let me into their lives. Well, let's see, I'm still in Scouts and we've become a pretty rockin' group. Got a happening planned tomorrow which I can't reveal, cause it's secret, if you know what I mean."

"Not really, Auti, but keep talking."

"Okay. The troop is so cool. We've a girl from California who was, get this, raised by wolves."

"Wow. Who shows up in Sugar City from So-Cal? Wolves?"

"Yeah. Some kind of motorcycle gang. Ana Estrella Story. I like her a lot. Plus, we got Maddy Weber..."

"Wait. That's right, Madison is in your troop." For Summer, the name triggered a flood of memories.

"Yeah. The other day she..."

Summer butted in, "She was our team manager, Auti."

Autumn pictured her sister becoming more animated.

"Weber was great, always kept us loose. Whatever we did our senior year, she played a big part. She was headstrong, and I doubt she's changed much. Hanging with Maddy is a good thing, sis. I'm glad you two are friends."

"At school this week she told us a lot about Coach Zaro and the team."

"Don't get me started. Every time I think about Coach I well up. Listen, can I tell you a quick story?"

"Sure."

"Gosh, I haven't thought about this in years. Anyway, it was early in the season and we weren't playing so hot. We traveled west to play the Murray Mustangs in an out-of-conference game, and man, we got trounced. After the thrashing, we're all sitting in the locker room tired and embarrassed, when Coach Zaro starts this tirade. I guess she just hit the wall in frustration. We were seniors. We had expectations. Anyway, Coach rants on and on and we're all rattled cause we'd never seen her like this. She finishes up by hollering at the ceiling, *And I'm so damn tired of being blown out!!* Right then you could hear an eyelash drop in that locker room. No one breathed. Then Maddy slowly saunters on over, puts her hand on Coach's shoulder and says, 'Well Ms. Zaro, I guess they played like candles in the wind.' The whole team blew up in hysterics. Coach was laughing the hardest of all."

"That sounds just like her."

"Ohhh, I'm so glad you and Madison have hooked up in Scouts. Can't wait to catch up with her this summer."

"That you will, big sis. Good luck with finals and..." Autumn struck a flirtatious chord. "Hey, Hot Stuff, say *hi* to Dexter for me."

"Very funny, Cool Down, I'm sure Mr. Longbridge will return the hello. I love you, little sister. Be safe. Bye."

"Love you back. Call me soon."

That night at supper, Dorothy tried to squeeze out as much info as she dared, particularly with regard to the mysterious Scout affair planned for tomorrow. Autumn knew the game well, and fended off her mom as best she could. She was saved when her gramps arrived. The intended overnight was nothing out of the ordinary. She stayed a lot with her grandparents.

Dorothy, exasperated, made one final try. "Land sake, there are times you and your sister can be so hush-hush."

"Well, Mother, Summer did swear to me one secret I simply can't keep."

"What's that, dear?"

Autumn leaned closer to her mom and in a fake whisper said, "She's now got a tattoo on her butt that reads...born to farm."

Her dad and gramps both shouted, "About time!"

Dorothy threw up her arms in frustration. "Gracious, Autumn Hook, what am I going to do with you?" Skewing her chuckling husband, "The two of you."

Autumn was up from the table and moving, grabbing her bag. "Don't ever change, Ma. Come on, Gramps. Love you both."

II
THE STORYS

Stirring a pasta concoction on the stove, Zeb grabbed the ringing phone. Had to be Ana. They had a pact of always checking in at night when apart. Normally he'd be missing her. He understood his daughter's close friendship with Rachel Bradbury as a good thing. The girls' overnights together were fine, but the house was so empty when she was gone. He loved yakking over the day's events, watching her animated face and listening to her lively voice; just the two of them. Zeb always carried the "ache"—what Rene was missing. How thrilled she'd be with their growing daughter.

But not tonight. Tonight he was whipping up a carbonara dish with lustful thoughts of Jessi Bradbury. This was new, shockingly new! He caught it on the third ring. "Yo."

"Calling to say goodnight, *Papi*."

"Okay Ana, sleep tight."

"Dad, before I hang, you were at Rachel's today… working…right?"

Zeb stopped stirring. Perplexed, he thought, Oh boy, here we go. Careful now. He imagined himself traipsing lightly across a frozen winter pond. "Affirmative."

"And?"

"And what, Ana?"

"You're holding out on me, *Papi.*"

Zeb heard the ice cracking beneath him. "Where are we going with this?"

"I'm smiling, *Papi.* I've a bemused look on my face. *Bemused,* that's my English vocab word this week at school. Phew! Finally found a place for it. Wanted you to know that."

Zeb laughed. "You were saying goodnight, right?"

Ana continued on like she wasn't listening. "It's just that Rachel caught her mom singing to herself tonight. And get this, whistling too."

"So?"

"Soooo, Rach says her mom hasn't sung in like forever. And whistling? Like, never."

Mimicking Ana's soooo, Zeb countered, "Whistling and singing, that's good, right?"

"I need you to toss me a ringer here, *Papi.* No secrets between us. House Rules. Remember?"

Zeb felt himself plunging into the icy water. Aww, the hell with it. Ana was right. No secrets. "Ms. Bradbury and I shared a *momento* this afternoon. I kissed her."

"No way!"

Zeb now surprised even himself. "Ready for another horseshoe?"

"I'm all ears, *Papi.*"

"Have you got a grip on something? This may come as a shock."

"I'm not even breathing, *Papi.*"

"She kissed me back...passionately."

"*¡Ay caramba!*"

"Night, Ana." With that, Zeb hung up the phone and laughed out loud like he hadn't in years. Oh, to be a fly on the wall in the Bradbury house tonight.

FRIDAY, MAY 11, 2001

Low-level cumulus clouds sweep across the Missouri River and on into Iowa; the fast-moving cold mass collides with and undercuts the sheet of warm moist air expanding northward from the Gulf region. Generated updrafts of warm air expand and explode into the stratosphere.

12
THE TROOP

Jessi Bradbury was up early. Fitful dreams of Zeb kept her tossing and turning half the night. What had she started? She knew without asking that she was lonely (and admit it, girl—horny as hell), but never believed she'd throw caution and reserve off a cliff. Maintaining a modicum of control was a source of pride. How had she completely lost that with one kiss from Zeb? Plus, denying everything to Rachel and Ana was stupid. Zeb was right about that. Peppering questions, they'd had her off balance all evening. Now, today, seeing Zeb again, what to think? There was a sea of possibilities. Jessi almost smiled to herself. Suddenly life was full of mischief.

Checking, she found the two of them already gone; off to a half-recollected super-early school project. With all the fur flying last night concerning Mr. Story, the girls' plans had gotten lost in the shuffle.

Twenty minutes later, Jessi was in aisle 2 at the grocery, scanning cereal boxes for in-store sales when her cart collided with another. Wanda Derry looked up and smiled apologetically. "Sorry, Jessi. Good day to you. Mercy," she was fanning herself with the local newspaper, "feels like August."

Jessi returned the smile. "Hi, Wanda. I know. Summer's arrived like a February robin. Bit early."

They passed by one another when Wanda turned and said casually, "Good to see your Scouts out and about so early this morning."

Jessi felt a tingling of alarm, then attempted to hide her misgivings by nonchalantly musing, "Let's see, what's on tap for today? Where did you see them?"

"Oh, I had to help out with Jed's paper route this morning. Up and out at the crack of dawn, as usual. We passed by them up near the old Snethen place, southeast end of town. They were walking together in uniform, lugging backpacks and cardboard signs. They all waved and smiled as we drove by. That Rachel of yours is such a fine young gal. She's already a beauty." With a gleam in her eye, Wanda asked, "You got your troop out on an early-bird secret mission?"

"Bless you, Wanda. You're so very kind." Jessi barely got the words out, her mind racing. They couldn't. They wouldn't! How had she been so blind? Silently cursing, she instantly knew what they were up to: Madison's mission at the Scout meeting—the trees. Anxiety growing, she said, "The Scouts, yes, you've reminded me, Wanda. I've got to rush off. You have a fine day now, you hear?" Backtracking, she reshelved a few items from her cart, left the rest, and walked quickly to the automatic exit, then sprinted to her car.

———

Madison Weber was having second thoughts. If she'd planned better, they all might have ridden bikes to the park. Lugging school stuff, the signs, and backpacks would have been a pain but doable. Of course, Lily didn't own a bike, but why not just borrow one? This whole goofball plan of having Autumn hijack her gramps's flatbed was ripe for disaster. She felt on edge. Yet, here they were, having met up as intended, happily walking together to the designated rendezvous. Only a few early risers had passed them by. Folks waved and they all waved back, giving no cause for alarm—so far. She was half-listening in as Ana and Rachel talked excitedly of a mom, a dad, and a passionate kiss. The four of them rounded a bend in the road and—there she was. Wow! Auti stood alongside the truck, teasingly tapping her foot and checking her watch—big smile.

Special school projects provided easy excuses to slip away from home early. Lily, Ana, and Rachel had all set out with parental encouragement. Their lies might come back to haunt them, but right now, tossing their homemade signs and backpacks on the truck bed, they resembled a gaggle of young geese clamoring and climbing into the front cab. The long vinyl seat was able to accommodate all five. This was heady stuff; a real adventure.

"Ready, troop?" Autumn shouted.

"You sure you know how to operate this rig?" Lily asked, her pale blue eyes radiating apprehension.

Autumn smiled. "I've only bounced it around on the farm, so this is a first, being on public roads and all. You better grab hold tight, Lil."

Jiggling the long floor shifter into neutral, Autumn pressed her foot down on the starter and gas pedal, igniting the lumbering beast. A cheer went up as she ground gears into first and got the truck rolling. Rachel gave Ana a hug. "I can't believe we're doing this!"

They didn't have far to drive, perhaps a couple miles using side streets to navigate around town before reaching the state highway and the final leg to the plant. The plan was to get to Wildnut first, stash the truck on a long abandoned park service road, and make their stand at the north-side entrance.

Cautiously rounding street corners, Madison was praying they'd avoid a police patrol car, or worse—parents. Thinking warily, *This is going far too easy,* she was suddenly lurched forward along with everyone else when Autumn, surprised by two early morning joggers heading directly toward them in the street, slammed on the brakes while failing to depress the clutch in time, and stalled the old flatbed to a sputtering halt.

Stalling out proved to be the least of their problems. The two runners were high school senior jocks, Kurt Blue and Sal somebody. The boys stopped, looked on in amazement, playfully elbow-jabbed each other in the ribs, then strolled over to the passenger cab window casting leery grins inside. The girls, their exhilaration gone, shriveled up, not risking a glance at the two intruders.

"Where all you illegals headin'?"

Autumn managed a reply. "No business of yours."

The two boys, cocky smiles, were loving this. "Little early for joy riding, ain't it?"

"Yeah, listen up, jail bait. Yer suppose to jack a hot sports car, not some milk wagon."

The guys high-fived one another, busting up.

Madison silently and urgently mouthed, *Get it going!* to Autumn.

"Kinda young for a learner's permit, ain't ya?"

"Good thing you're along, Hook. I'm not sure the rest of 'em can see over the steering wheel."

Leave it to Lily, sitting crammed up against the window, to lead the counter-attack. "Eeeee...yew, when was the last time you guys took a shower?" The boys turned indignant, scowling, "Hey! Watch your mouth, pipsqueak. It's hot as hell runnin' out here." Kurt, leaning close, fanned his sweat-soaked jersey at her.

No one noticed Kurt's younger brother Riley, panting and near out of breath, jog into view. Without hearing a word, he knew exactly how this scene was playing out.

"About time you caught up," Kurt smirked. "You expect to play varsity ball this summer, you best find another gear, bro."

Riley ignored the put-down. "Leave them alone, K. You too, Sal. Get gone; the both of you. The Yanks and Bo-Sox await."

The boys backed off. Kurt, pointing to Madison, joked, "Yer girlfriend here is running away from home and dragging all her friends with her. Lasso that palomino, eh little brother?"

"Stuff it, Kurt."

Kurt Blue stared down his younger brother. "Okay, Romeo, but I want to see your butt in the weight room this morning."

Riley nodded. "I'm right behind you. Now beat it."

Sal tapped his partner on the shoulder and jerked his thumb back toward the school. The two spun around and jogged off.

Lots of exhales escaped from inside the truck cab.

"Way to go, Lily," Ana said. "You zinged them good. *Muchacha valiente.*"

Rachel was nudging Autumn. They smiled at one another, then sang out: "Hiii, Riley." Madison gave them both an evil eye.

Riley Blue was watching the backs of his brother and Sal trail off. Hearing his name, he turned and strolled to the truck. As if nothing had happened, as if no one else existed, he butted up against the passenger door. "Hey, Madison."

She didn't look up, but did manage a whispered, "Hey, Riley," in return. *My God*, she thought, *those guys—and now this. A disaster churning into a catastrophe.*

Riley was aware, at last, of the five girls crammed together. "Any of you have an older brother? If not, you are so lucky. Sorry about the Neanderthals." He was speaking to them all, but his focus never strayed from Madison. "Riding around for kicks? Heading somewhere?"

"Wildnut Park," Lilly answered.

Riley cocked his head. "That old place? Scout thing?"

Ana nodded. "Pretty close."

Riley dropped the subject. He'd been hoping to share his recent good fortune. Here was an unexpected chance. "Guess what, Madison, you know Hamilton's repair shop, right? He offered to hire me maybe full time this summer. Pretty cool, huh? Alex says you stop by. Maybe we could hang around together."

Madison made no reply.

Taking advantage of the Blue/Weber stilted stand-off, Rachel, with pen and paper in hand, hurriedly and discretely inked out a sign.

Riley was blowing his chance. He knew it. Maddy Weber always made him nervous and tongue-tied. They were never going to connect. "Wildnut Park? Feels like a scorcher today. You guys all got water?"

Everyone nodded, save Weber, whose hand flew and covered her mouth. "Oh gosh, I forgot. I can't believe it!"

Riley gallantly unsheathed his own water from a belt holder. "Here, take mine. I've just a short ways to go." Thrusting the plastic bottle through the window, Madison reached over and took it, saying quietly, "Thanks Riley, appreciate it."

Sitting to Madison's left, Rachel and Autumn saw their chance and held up Bradbury's hastily scrawled message: **CALL HER!** all the while silently pointing to their bashful compatriot.

Riley smiled, "Look, I've got to run, literally. See you in class, Madison. Be careful, all."

Letting go his firm grip on the cab door, he spun and jogged off, but not before his ears caught the four-girl *Byeeee, Riley* gleeful shout. He slowed to wave and saw that Madison had leaned over past Lily and had his water bottle waving back at him. Okay, he thought, grinning, Did something right. How cool is that.

In the truck, Madison surveyed her giggling idiot friends. "Squash the Greek chorus, will ya?"

She may as well have been lecturing the wind. One-liners floated around her.

"Total dreamboat."

"Riley's like so Brad."

"Did you see the starry-eyed look he gave her?"

"More like a drool."

Rachel emoted, "Madd, your complexion, your hair...so dark. Riley's all fair and blond. I wonder..."

Madison nearly leaped at her. "Don't even think, Bradbury." Pounding the dash to stop the cackling, she pleaded, "I'm new at this stuff, okay? Look at you, Rachel. Half the boys in our class become lap dogs whenever you walk by. God, some fool dangled from the overpass bridge out on the highway to paint 'I love Rachel' for the whole world to see, and you don't even know who it was."

"There are lots of Rachels, Maddy."

"Oh *right*, for sure. Thing is, I don't know how to act, so stop teasing me. You're making it hard. Stop teasing us. We can find our own way, if he likes me. I don't know why. I'm an only child and still the runt of the litter."

Rachel had heard enough. "First off, Webslinger, Riley and you are the two shyest human beings on the planet, so a little prodding can't hurt. He's got a big-time crush on you. We've all seen it. And it's like you want to, but you don't hardly react at all. Second, goofball, if we can't tease each other about boys, we are totally messed up. Besides, we all know you like him big time."

"We just want you to see yourself in the mirror the way we see you," Autumn said. "You put yourself down too much. I mean, obviously, Riley thinks you're a sexy runt."

"Mark my words, *amiga*," Ana said, "you are in for a rockin' summer."

Madison rolled her eyes. "Thanks a bunch, guys." But she couldn't help but smile. Deep down she was cheered.

"At least someone has taken an interest," Lily piqued. "Check me out. The skinny BP."

"BP?" Madison asked.

"Me! The boobless pipsqueak."

Madison, Ana, Rachel, and Autumn roared with laughter. Lily was far from being consoled. Staring down at the floorboard, she said, "You heard those two guys, it's the truth."

"Ratsafrats," Madison scolded, giving her friend a huge hug. "With all this beautiful blond hair, you're blossoming like a yellow rose, Lil. A bona fide late-blooming heartbreaker."

"Yeah."

"Got that right."

"You are a BP," Autumn added, "and it stands for beautiful person, Lily Starr."

Ana startled the troop. "Hey! *Soldados!* Blossoming? Don't we have trees to save?"

Without further incident, Autumn manhandled the flatbed to Wildnut Park. Getting close they realized to their utter dismay the tree cutters had already arrived.

"Too late. Maybe we oughta turn back."

"Bull frog, Madd. Hang on, troop." Autumn didn't hesitate. Gripping the steering wheel for dear life she gunned the old Ford, turning down an incline on what Madison later described as nothing more than a moon cratered dirt trail. The girls grew wild-eyed and braced for calamity as Autumn bounced the truck through and around equipment, raising a thick cloud of dust in the process. Lumberjacks scattered in every direction. At the last, with her heart racing, and far too heavy on the breaks, she orchestrated a four-tire sliding screeching stop—somehow exactly at the planned spot. Five rag dolls disembarked, practically falling from the cab, blissfully thanking the All-merciful above for a safe journey's end.

Holding their collective breath, eyes straight ahead, Troop 822 proceeded through the trees, past the puzzled work crew, sequestering themselves in full view on the grassy hillside between the towering oaks and the Heartland factory. Their made-up signs read:

TREE KILLERS
SAVE THE PARK—YOU'LL BE SO SORRY
and Madison's personal admonition to the axe men:
CHAINSAW YOUR LIFE!

Having survived Autumn's wild entrance, Lonnie
Shimmer's boys regrouped, pointed, and looked on in
amusement. Lonnie himself was scratching his scalp,
muttering, "What in the hell?"

On the hillside, the Scouts realized their worst fears. It
was all but over. Their odyssey to save the park was down the
tubes. Despite protesting with passion and rage, all they really
had was a front-row seat to watch the oaks being cut down.
Madison was at a loss, feeling physically sick, when instinctively
she faced north, and observed a KBOX-TV van turn onto the
entrance road. She nudged the others, pointing. "Guys. Look!
Over there. Maybe a ray of hope."

13
THE NEWS CREW

Kelly Bauer released her seat belt and stepped down from the Channel 6 News van. Canvassing about, her heart sank. Not yet seven a.m., and already in amongst the timber the lumbermen stood at ease stretching and drinking coffee. Bucket trucks, pickups, and dozers were parked nearby, shimmering in the bright morning sunshine. Three of the men, one with chainsaw in hand, were examining the northernmost oak. The tree was huge; a great white, soaring one hundred feet high, sporting limbs that begged for a tree-house. Kelly's outstretched arms wouldn't reach halfway around the silo-sized trunk.

Set apart from the other two dozen trees composing the grove, the old oak stood like a sentinel guarding and protecting the regiment, its branches blowing *Reveille* and *Taps* each day for the past one hundred years. Blocking the heavy equipment from entering the park, the majestic white stood to be the first tree destroyed.

Kelly's survey swept east to a hillside where the so-called demonstrators had gathered. They were wearing school

clothes with brown vests and raising up homemade paper
signs too distant to read. The so-called protest amounted to
a horsefly on a Clydesdale's rump, guaranteed to be swatted
away once the chainsaws and idling dozers began to labor.

From her vantage point beside the parked van, the scene
represented her worst fear: a nonstory. She recalled a few years
back how her dad had scoffed at her majoring in journalism.
Long hours and low pay, he'd insisted, even pointing out the
ever-possible danger. You can go from Main Street, USA, to
Mogadishu in an eyelash of ambition.

She'd defended her choice, believing she possessed
that special sense, a reporter's nose for the undetected and
unexpected. Now, here outside Sugar City, having already
burned a few bridges, perhaps putting her KBOX internship
on the line, she was left filled with doubt. Doubt that was
rapidly giving way to anxiety.

Where were the barricades, the outraged citizens, the
embattled, outnumbered law enforcement officers? Where
were the Greens, the environmental extremists squatting aloft
or chained to the doomed trees? Where was the overpowering
smell of drifting tear gas? Kelly flung her arms skyward in a
mocking gesture. What is this? A few middle-school teens and
a bunch of half-awake farm boys! Holy hell's bells, I'm in *big*
trouble. She horse-laughed over her plight while totaling up
IOU's accrued (and stay real, girl—the flat-out lies told) to
arrive on location this morning. How in the hell had she ever
allowed this to happen? Oh yeah, simple, as she reconstructed

the thought process and events that led to this job ending screw-up.

"Okay, follow up more on the phone. Track down our Voice of Reason caller. Put together a wrap-up piece. Maybe we can find a weekend time slot, or cradle it with another small town saga on down the line. Keep me posted, Bauer."

Joan Chase provided a sliver of daylight. Kelly hatched a plan, inventive and reckless. The Sugar City Story felt worth the risk. She thought Chase had been purposely vague. What were her instructions? Track down. Yes, her very words and—the young caller had pleaded for prevention, not some reportage after the fact. Kelly was poised to run at this story. All she needed were a couple of blockers.

Kelly had been at her network summer dream job a mere three weeks. That partial first month provided adequate time for photographer Joey Rockland to develop a crush. No way was she encouraging that—but suddenly on Thursday, May 10, sweet Joey was this huge asset.

Pulling on heartstrings and hustling Joey into joining forces was going to be delicate. Rolling on down to Sugar City in a commandeered KBOX-TV microwave van loomed nigh impossible. And yet—Joey's best bud at the station just happened to be sound engineer/van operator, Roberto Tavares.

Kelly's mind was a six-speed tranny, shifting gears clicking into place. "Maybe," she murmured softly. "Just maybe."

Luckily, Joey was in-house. Kelly stalked him down, hooked her right arm with his left and said, "We need to chat." Over coffee she explained her ideas for reporting the story. She fought for his support with the best ammunition she had: the truth. That driving to Sugar City in a stuffy corporate sedan, taping a few interviews from both sides *after* the sawdust settled; some folk in tears over the destroyed trees, others spewing about the importance of jobs, progress, and the big picture; then driving back, editing, splicing in the before-and-after shots, hoping for fifteen seconds on the Ten, just wasn't going to freaking cut it. She reached across the table and took hold of Joey's hand. Giving him her best doe-eyed look, she made a case for being on-location early tomorrow with one of the station's microwave vans, the impact of reporting the story as events unfolded, and scooping the other metro networks.

Joey wasn't impressed. "You're letting ambition overrule common sense, Bauer. You're what...two weeks in? You're a rook. Chase won't turn you loose on your own. Run off with a microwave? To Sugar City? Who ya kiddin'? I don't even know where the town is, but chances are slim we'd be able to hook up live. This is crazy...and why are you holding my hand?"

Kelly went to Plan B. "There's an immediacy to this story, Joey: unchecked development, rural small town confrontation, the plight of Iowa's natural resources." Her hoped-for photog shook his head. "No! You're a fruitcake. Forget it." He spied his watch and began to make excuses to leave.

A pretty face and down-home honesty weren't enough.

Plan C was a last hope. Kelly knew Joey and Roberto longed to be storm chasers. Get a couple of beers in 'em and talk inevitably shifted to twisters: catching one on film—a wedge, not a rope—a big one—level 5. Their eyes lit up exchanging tales, the shared bravado over near-misses.

Before Joey made his exit, Kelly edged in close enough to kiss him. She whispered, "Weather-lab reports southeastern Iowa will be under a tornado watch tomorrow morning. Hardcastle County looks to be the ripe spot. All hell could break loose down there."

Kelly saw Joey Rockland's eyes flicker, registering and measuring the pros and cons. He gave her a quick peck on the cheek. "I'll call Roberto tonight. See what's shakin'."

KBOX meteorologist Monty Ammerman huddled with assistants, scanning the latest satellite and radar weather data. Now four a.m., they'd been working all night. The stationary front in southern Iowa was, at this moment, under assault by two air masses rocketing in from the Northern Rockies and the Gulf of Mexico. The latest Doppler posting brought a cold chill. Thunderstorms produce the most violent weather on Earth. Conditions laid bare the possibility of the fronts colliding into a perfect storm.

New gal Kelly Bauer popped her head into the lab, breaking Monty's concentration. "Burning the midnight oil, eh Mr. Ammerman?"

Monty smiled. "Early morning fire, Ms. Bauer?"

"Maybe. Riding down Sugar City way to check on a story. Keep the sun shining, Mr. Ammerman."

As she waved to leave, Monty called out after her. "Ms. Bauer!"

Kelly stopped in her tracks, noting the alarm in his voice. "Yo."

Monty caught her eye. "Best keep a close watch on the sky this morning."

——————

Well, Monty was hours ago, and now here she was, adrift in cattle country, under a vomit-orange sky, with a hijacked microwave broadcast truck, second guessing disgruntled tech support, and her journalism career swirling down the toilet.

She swiftly glanced at Joey. *Playing the romance card?* What had she been thinking? And absconding the KBOX van—good Lord!—it had been almost too easy. She exhaled a short, manic laugh. Yeah, like no cub reporter had ever been stupid enough to even *try* to pull such a stunt. She knew she had the looks and smarts for this game. The camera had adored her since she was five. Where the hell was the patience? The idea of coming clean with Joey and Roberto, that she had *zero* authorization for this excursion, made her shudder. Her chewing-out and dismissal back at KBOX was going to be deserved, unpleasant, and permanent.

Okay, girl, she sighed, time to face the...Kelly stopped mid-thought to silently watch a car pull wildly into Heartland

and race past their van on down to the employee parking
lot. A woman leaped from the small hatchback and began
waving and making her way toward the Scouts. Then, a
guttural roar snapped Kelly's head 180 degrees as a half-dozen
motorcycles crested the northern ridge overlooking the park.
Harley Davidsons, idling roughly like snorting angus bulls,
formed in a line side-by-side. Riders, dressed in black leather
wearing colorful bandanas, loomed like the cavalry from the
underworld. Reacting instinctively, as any top-notch television
reporter might have, given the circumstances, she screamed
over the top of the chainsaws and revving cycles, *"Joey! Grab the
camera!!"*

14
THE BLUES

My backup plan was now in effect. Damn. I'd schemed
to have us all deployed early before anyone else showed.
Stonewall the lumberjacks, call in the cops, and create enough
tension and confusion to put the sacking of Wildnut at least on
hold. We needed time to allow more voices and viewpoints to
chime-in on this rogue roadwork. But we were late, nearly too
late, and plan A was by the boards.

Assembling the Dry Dogs anywhere is no easy task.
Freewheelin Ribbs was last to arrive at the shop, roaring in
regretful. And he brought his ferret for God's sake. Apparently
Red had been sleeping in a different place and was hard to
find, thus the delay. Okay, next!

Robin too was late. Wayne was on duty and one of the kids
awoke with a rash. Spider bite? Poison Ivy? The measles? Who
knew. Next!

On top of everything else, Harlin and Robin had this weird
vibe going on. We were at the shop waiting on Will, and the
two of them are dancing around one another like summer
moths circling a porch night-light. Harlin says, "I didn't intend

to kiss you again. The first one, well, I saw my chance and went ahead. It was meant as a beholden. The second kiss just happened."

Dry Dog's jaws dropped. What the?

Robin snapped, "You knew I might turn to face you. You took advantage."

Harlin smiled shyly. "Maybe."

Robin took notice our collective big ears and deadpanned, "Long story. Don't ask."

What a start to the campaign. Lost ferrets, sick kids, and a forbidden romance. Was Alexander the Great hassled with rank and file problems like this?

"You're the kingpin, Hamilton, bark out some orders." Zeb's exhortation was a shot of adrenalin. We had arrived. Better late than never. I envisioned what lay before us: The oaks, Shimmer's crew, the Scouts. Only the KBOX-TV van was a surprise. How and why were questions for a later date. I hollered at Ribbs, "Freewheelin. Tidings from the bard. I'm looking for a little moral support here."

Ribbs surveyed the park scene below us, deadpanning, "We could die down here, be just another accident statistic."

"No comfort there, Will," Zeb rendered, shouting over the rumbling bikes. Refocusing, he pointed at me. "What have you got for us, Commander?"

Just do it, I screamed silently to myself. Waving wildly at the north end of the grove, I charged, "Zeb, you and Harlin stop the chainsaw. They'll have that first oak downed in a flash. Put a halt to it. Nothing dies out here. Not today. *Move!*"

With a fleeting nod of acceptance, the two kicked their bikes into low, juiced the throttle, and roared off.

I leaned closer to Robin's, Gordon's, and Will's expectant faces, hollering, "Rest of us are going to corral those Scouts into the park. We need to spook them. Get 'em on the run."

"What?" Robin was alarmed, not quite comprehending.

"Like rustling cattle, Emerson. Follow me, then fan out as we approach. Gordon, take the left flank. Ribbs, you're on the right. Robin and I will block up the middle. Use your bikes. Funnel them toward the oaks. *Go! Go! Go!*"

And off we went. My tactical maneuver started well then turned to misadventure. We certainly gave Madison and her friends a fright; four snarling motorcycles barreling down on them, Robin and I pointing to the trees while screaming at the top of our lungs: "Move! Move!" Thankfully, they didn't scatter. Finding safety in numbers, they huddled up, grasped hands, and ran as one toward the oak grove. Following close behind, I heard their panic stricken voices, watched them stumble and fall, then be swiftly hoisted back up by those still afoot. With each recovery, their pace to reach the trees quickened. Though being hounded by four snarling motorcycles, no one was going to be left behind, not with this group. Alongside me, Robin too gave a yelp. Out of the corner of my eye I witnessed her lose control from the rough terrain. Bike and rider went sprawling. Mercy. Ankle sprains and bloody knees were one thing, but being jettisoned from a running-wild Harley Sportster was major. With my heart skipping beats, I grabbed a handful of brake and slid to a stop. Looking back, she was already back on her feet. Using the downgrade for leverage, and with a grunt, she expertly had the Sportster back on it's wheels. Ribbs too saw her wipe out, but by the time he'd raced over to assist, she had the Harley restarted, signaled him a thumbs up, and returned to the chase. Score one for Robin, the 'gamer'.

In the noise and confusion the kids had forgotten their gear, but Gordon stopped and managed to bungee up water bottles and back packs. What seemed like hours took mere minutes. Herded into the park, the Scouts hovered around an old picnic table, staying close, fearful eyes searching for explanation. We encircled them, then sprung kickstands and shut down the machines. Exhale. We were among the hardwood, without serious incident or injury. I hoped.

"Okay?"

Coated in dust and dirt, Robin had a face full of scorn. "Side views broke and bent all to hell. God knows what else."

"Not the bike! You."

"I'm *fine!* Jesus, Alex, what are we doing?"

"Not sure yet." With Robin still in one piece, I turned to our panting captives. Madison, squinting, provided me a look of recognition. I gave a little wave and smiled. She too exhaled and began to realize that Troop 822 would survive another day.

Before any of us were able to catch a breath, our attention was diverted to the confrontation on the north side. Both bikes were down. Zeb was up limping, but Harlin was sprawled on his back in obvious pain. Racing hard to rescue the tree being chain sawed, his motorcycle had jack-knifed, flipped, and lay twisted in a heap nearby. One of the lumberjacks was hurt; sitting on his butt with his back against the tree, wincing in agony. We heard lots of yelling, lots of threats. Estey left our group and ran to lend a hand.

"What the hell you nut cases think you're doin'? Jesus! Benny! Call 911. Get the sheriff out here. Tell 'em we need an ambulance. Milo's leg is hurt real bad. Damn." Lonnie Shimmer was blistering hot—"Jesus, what in hell, Shifter? Benny! Call Heartland. I want Dick Lester here pronto. *Now,* Benny!"—pacing about the intruders; pointing fingers. "You two cowboys are in deep shit. Harlin, you goddamn maniac."

Shifter, aided by Zeb, struggled to his feet. In pain and hanging on to Story's shoulder, he snapped back at Shimmer. "Pack up, Lonnie. Tell your timber rats to back off. The party's over. You listening to me? This operation is dead-ass over."

Enraged, Lonnie directed his boys to grab and hold the two bikers, but when Gordon Estey emerged from the shaded grove, everyone took a step back.

Zeb hollered. "I'll need that ambulance doc for Harlin here too, Lonnie."

"He needs a straitjacket. The hoodlum caused this mess. He can live with the damn consequences."

"That's it, Shim-shit. I ain't going nowhere." Fighting mad, fighting pain, Shifter ordered Zeb, "Get us together with the rest of them." Aiding each other, the three Dry Dogs, maintaining a wary eye on the tree crew, shuffled slowly backward into the grove. The young loggers looked relieved.

"Knew this job had cow crud shoveled all over it. TV cameras. Crazy bikers. Felt it all along." Shimmer was left befuddled. "Girl Scouts? Jesus. Dammit Benny, where's the cops? Where's Lester? God damn, Benny. I knew it."

Gordon piggy-backed Harlin to our shaded enclave. Ribbs got him halfway comfortable lying down on top of a picnic table. Will's diagnosis was not good.

Shifter's chopper was built along classic lines. Seat perched low on the frame. Peanut tank bolted on high. Before catapulting over his bike, Rat Tail Shifter had crushed his chest against the gas tank. Will was certain that Harlin's ribs were broken. He also had a severe leg gash that needed stitching.

We tore T-shirts into pressure bandages to get the bleeding stopped. I offered up my riding back brace and our doc put it to good use wrapping and strapping the leg to help seal the wound, all the while commanding his patient to lie still, warning Harlin that a rib fracture might puncture a lung. Mercy. I was glad Ribbs was with us.

After being stampeded, Troop 822 was calming. The motorcycles sat parked. The chain saws were still. A welcome quiet prevailed, but not for long. Any hope of molding this gathering together was quickly dashed as the two groups stared in stunned recognition. I'm wishful thinking: *Say hi to your dad, Ana. Rachel, here comes mom. Be nice and say hello.*

Disheveled, exhausted, carrying a broken shoe, Jessi Bradbury staggered into the grove after a long run from the parking lot. The look on her sweat-strewn face would spawn shivers in a nest of vampires. She lashed out first at daughter Rachel, then focused her full rage at Zeb, who was, at the time, chewing out poor Ana. In their defense, both girls only managed a "but-but-but" during the parental tirades. They probably felt relief when the grownups (and at this point I use the term loosely) verbally pounced on one another. Ms. troop leader launched the opening salvo.

"What in *God's name* are you up to?"

Zeb was in no mood for argument. Beat up and sore from his tumble off the bike, concerned for Shifter, incredulous at discovering his daughter Ana involved, he steamrolled an answer. "You don't know jack what's going on here, lady! Quit overreacting! I've got problems of my own."

"Overreacting?! You...you...ass! I witnessed what you did. You nearly ran over the kids with those motorcycles. Overreacting! I lost a husband to a freak accident. You...you... numbnut!!" Jessi was breathing hard and rapidly, fists clenched close to her sides. "This is *my* Scout troop. They are *my* responsibility. I'm a wee bit on the *protective* side here, Mister Story!"

Our esteemed president's reply didn't help matters. "Wait just a darned minute. Numbnut? What is that? Mister? I thought we'd agreed to a first-name basis."

Dumbfounded, Jessi let go a, "grrrrahhhhhhhhhhhh."

Ana finally got a word in edgewise. "I don't think that was the answer she was looking for, *Papi*."

Marching straight at him, Jessi was set to throw a haymaker to the chin or swing a swift kick to the shin, maybe both.

Right then, Autumn and Rachel cried out: "We're all on the same side."

Jessi stopped dead in her tracks. The declaration caught everyone by surprise, allowing a moment to take stock. Bickering was silenced. We stood shuffling our feet. All was quiet. The tree branches themselves waved a sigh of relief.

I said matter-of-factly, "We're here to save the oaks."

The Scouts reacted in unison. "So are we!"

Police sirens were wailing in the background. I regarded them all. "We need a plan."

Ana bent an ear, noting the sirens getting closer. *"Sí, rapido."*

15
THE NEWS CREW

"Color me Cronkite. Joey, did you get all that?" Kelly Bauer stood transfixed, astonished. "Did we just witness a kidnapping? Did you capture those motorcycles going down; that guy flipping...those kids running and screaming...you think we got some kind of hostage situation here?"

"Got it all, chief."

Kelly nodded. "Let's try to talk to the guy in charge of the tree crew. Find out what he knows. What a crazy situation. You think those Scouts are in real danger here, Joey? Maybe if we hike down into the tree grove..."

"Hold on a minute, Kelly." Joey realized he had to slow his young colleague down. "We're reporting the story, not taking part. We're too far to make out all the yelling. All's quiet right now. Better we sit tight for now."

"Right. Let's interview this, what's his name...wait a sec. Can we go *live* with this? Roberto! Can we go *live*?!"

The two techs exchanged questioning glances. "We're too far from base," Roberto Tavares acknowledged, then laughed. "Next time, *senorita*, hi-jack the satellite truck." He grew serious. "We might connect with the KMAG tower at Davenport. This time of day. Early enough. Bird-time probably be available. We'll need lady luck. Worth a shot."

Joey, comprehending, instructed Kelly, "Get on the cell with whoever's producing this morning. Have them call and coordinate with our Quad City sister station. We'll tape and edit at our end. With an uplink and bounce off the satellite, home-base will have our stuff within the half hour. You want this story on the box? Start setting it up, Bauer!"

The KBOX crew got busy. Wireless connections clicked. Charmed hook-ups were finalized. Kelly noted the time. "We've got your pictures, Joey. We need an intro. A voiceover. I'll be damned, we might still make the Seven."

"Maybe. I'm way ahead of you, Bauer. Get primed. I need a second to set poles and flags. We've got an eerie light here."

"Forget the lighting! Damn, Joey, we're in overdrive. I'll just wing it." She closed her eyes, seeking a moment of composure. Her erstwhile story had risen from the basement freezer to the kitchen broiler in a ten-minute span. So much was happening so fast there was no time to think. "Oh God, Joey, what's my opening?"

He smiled, advising, "Take a deep breath. How about...A peaceful protest took on a bizarre twist this morning. Remember, Kelly, we've got editing capabilities. Make a mistake or lose your train of thought...don't fret. Back track. Keep it tight. You're earning your stripes here, Bauer."

Tavares was thumbs-up.

"Okay." Joey was set. "We're rolling."

KBOX NEWSROOM: NEWSDESK AT THE SEVEN

"We have late-breaking news to relay to station viewers this morning. KBOX reporter Kelly Bauer is on the scene outside Sugar City in southeast Iowa. Kelly?"

"I'm here, Patrick. What began as a peaceful protest over cutting down trees in a rural park took on a bizarre twist just before seven a.m. as a gang of motorcyclists sent a small band of Girl Scouts running for their lives..."

"...Right now, no word has been heard from the wooded area. I understand medical personnel and police are on the way. I can hear sirens in the background. "

Juliet Spinnetti was crossing through the Drake University Student Center, yawning and aiming downstairs for the much-desired coffee urn, when the unmistakable voice of her roomie boomed from the TV nook. "Hey Spinster, ain't your loverboy from down around Sugar City? You better come have a look at this."

Juliet detoured on in, plumped down on the couch, and joined a few early risers catching the morning news.

"...chaotic situation. To repeat, five young Girl Scouts appear to have been abducted by a band of motorcyclists. The Scouts were here apparently protesting the removal of a grove of oak trees at a park outside Sugar City, located in southeast Iowa. Police have just arrived at the scene. As soon as we learn more, we intend to provide additional pictures and commentary. This is Kelly Bauer, reporting live for KBOX at the..."

Fully awake now, Juliet stole a look at her roommate; all the while resurrecting the weird telephone conversation she'd had with Alex—when?—Wednesday last. The dots connected. "Holy shit!"

16
THE TROOP AND THE BLUES

The Scout's "We're all on the same side!" declaration shelved our discord a spell and allowed me to seize the pulpit. We had to jell right now. Owning up to Madison and her friends, I spoke out, "I'm looking at unfamiliar faces here, and I'm sure you're wondering who the heck we are. Problem is, we've no time for name-tags and round-robin introductions. Bottom line: we all want to save the trees in this park. Let's trust to that, and do what we can to support one another."

My opening gambit drew blank stares from the Scouts; their clothes smudged with dirt and grime, their faces blotched and dripping sweat. They'd gathered around Will Ribbs's bike, animated over the caged ferret, who, despite having taken part in my wild Napoleonic maneuver, appeared to have slept through the entire sortie. The rascal seemed to comfort them, but I was hip that there was a lot of teenage wariness left in these gals. "You are Sugar City Troop 822." I had my eye on Madison. She nodded. "And you have been chased into this grove by the Dry Dog Blues, the best-looking motorcycle club in these United States. Isn't that right, Rat Tail?"

Wincing in pain, Harlin Shifter managed a rather non-supportive, "Up yours, Straydog."

Taking a step closer toward the girls, I said with a wink, "Togetherness is our middle name."

Time was short. Standing straight and tall, trying to appear commanderish, I lashed together a plan. "First thing. Zeb. You just volunteered to confront our police chief. Make sure he's aware the girls are okay; that we've all banded together, that..." I hesitated. My reasoning was lurching about like one of those irritating music videos; patterned images and ideas changing every two seconds. "Hold on, Zeb. Don't say directly that we've joined forces. Just assure the chief the Scouts are safe and sound, that Jessi Bradbury is here with them. Explain we've got a man down who needs transport to the hospital." I observed him closely then scanned over to Robin, standing over by Harlin, gingerly nursing a sore something. "Maybe two or three. Plus, and this is vital, Zeb, he has to understand why we're hunkered down in the park. Ask for time. Ask him to leave us be awhile; that we're coming out to read a list of demands to end the stand-off. Don't let the cops dictate, Zeb. Keep 'em back on their heels."

"I'll go out there with him," Jessi said, "and help confirm things."

Jiminy. Jessi's offer was a tough one. I went with my gut. "No, no, only Zeb. Better they're confused out there. We need to maintain the mystery."

Guarded, bewildered faces eyed me from all directions. "Look, Rolli's going to want us out pronto. I'm positive that with all our snarls and snags, the trees won't be destroyed today. But we want a pledge the axe guys won't return tomorrow. We'll set terms. Nothing outrageous. Maybe a work stoppage for let's say...seven days. A proposal both sides can agree to."

"There has to be a town meeting where people like Mrs. Brackett at the library can have a say."

"Absolutely, Ms. Weber. A public referendum for saving the park." I gave her my best thank-you look.

Madison added, "We need a name."

"What?"

"For our group here. You know, like the Black Panthers or something."

I grinned. "You're right. A name might provide some focus," I added silently to myself, a hint that we're slightly organized, "but we are hardly the Black Panthers."

Jumping on Madison's suggestion, the Scouts began whispering and conspiring. They put their heads together, and an animated discussion ensued. At last, Autumn Hook nudged Lily Starr and said, "No, it's good. Go on. Ask."

Lily looked to her troop leader, shyly quizzing, "Ahhhh, Ms. Bradbury, what did you call him earlier?" She was pointing at Zeb.

Jessi had no time to answer. Ana, incensed over her dad's totally unfair tongue lashing, spoke out quickly. "She called him an ass." With flashing eyes she repeated, *"Una mula."*

Jessi stood aside confused.

Autumn said, "Yes, but that was because he called *her* something. Hmmmmm, what was that?"

Troop 822 was on a roll, tossing lines back and forth like a Chinese Ping-Pong match. Rachel was grinning from recognition. "I believe Mr. Story said something like, 'Hit the road, Jack.'"

"*That's it!*" They all shouted at once. Ana and Rachel slapped a high-five.

Zeb and Jessi lofted an eyebrow at one another and shrugged, clueless.

The girls had lost me, too. "That's what?" I asked.

Ana answered, "The name of our group. The Jackasses."

From the picnic table, Harlin moaned, "You got that right."

Lily spoke with furrowed brow. "No-no-no. Remember Auti yelling that we're on the same side?" She looked up expectantly. "So, that's like, allies, right?"

Will Ribbs and Autumn Starr said it first, together. "The Jackass Alliance."

We were promptly struck dumb; then the confirmation began.

"Fits this bunch."

"*A perfecto.*"

"Does have a righteous ring to it."

"Retro rad. Totally."

"Been called worse."

I had to admit. The girls offered up a sobriquet dressed in cosmic sense. "Done," I said. "And," eyeing Zeb and Jessi—

teasing them, "you two best be careful from now on what you say to each other."

Laughter aside, we had to go forward. "Take heed, people. A name's all we got. Zeb, go smoke the peace pipe with Rolli. The rest of us are going to hash out a pact to save these trees."

|7
THE CHIEF

Cradling a bullhorn in one hand, waving dismissal with the other, Sugar City Police Chief Roland Guy was doing his best to shed the pesky KBOX–TV reporter. Rolli needed answers, not questions. Normally a man known for his easy-going gait, Chief Guy was all take-charge and strictly business this morning.

He'd been an appointed small town flatfoot in Sugar City for two decades. Over the years, city mayors and city councils had come and gone. Rolli stayed put, his yearly job evaluations often piloting merit pay raises. He was a man who recognized circumstance and differentiated between the measure and the letter of the law. During his long tenure, more than a few wayward malcontents had been provided with a second chance, and they made good use of it. He was tough as cowhide, but fair. It was appreciated.

Getting on in years, Rolli had been struggling with his weight. Dr. Jolly's heart warnings concerning his expanding girth were a check-up forewarning received annually. His wife, Win, had him walking and dieting. She was after him to retire, fretting over the stresses that snaked about his job. Of late, the horrible meth-lab thing frightened her to the core. And Rolli, with seasoned thought, knew Win was right. Enough is enough. He'd catch himself spying in the mirror at his sagging long face and ever-expanding bulbous nose. He was looking more and more like his old saddle horse; stabled east of town. Horse and rider had been together many a year. Now, the two of them were trotting well past middle age, losing hair and gaining paunch—twins, for God's sake. At times, Rolli believed their only degree of separation was that he walked on two legs and Radar stomped about on four.

This morning wasn't helping his stress level. After years of beat-pounding out in the sticks and pasture, he'd swear he'd seen and heard it all. Earlier, while making rounds and preparing Sugar City for possible severe weather, Marge, on duty at county dispatch, was suddenly all over the radio, raving about a code 10-93 in progress at Wildnut Park. He'd been sitting in his squad car, contemplating cheating on his loyal and loving wife by stopping in and grabbing one of those huge cinnamon rolls that Larry baked and delivered each morning to the local service station. He was so close. But the urgent call kept the seat belt latched. He was baffled. What in the hell is a code 10-93? Marge needed to be weaned away from her TV cop shows.

Details ensued. Lonnie Shimmer had called in the 911: Harlin Shifter and Alex Hamilton and Girl Scouts and kidnapping and hostages and serious injuries and TV reporters.

It was all the dark side on the moon. Rolli was a blank slate. The ride over provided a few minutes to collect thoughts and make sense of the scattered report. He'd known both boys their whole lives. Shifter was a huge chip on the shoulder, but neither he nor Hamilton were apt to go haywire and cross on over into oncoming traffic. He'd bet his career on it.

There had to be a reasonable explanation, *but* (and this is what rubbed him raw) there was an obvious current flowing through Sugar City that had swept past him. A golden rule in law enforcement is "avoid surprises." How in blazes is a TV studio, from one hundred-plus miles away, more tuned into the goings-on in Sugar City than his department? Totally unacceptable! As he arrived and was turning onto Heartland's factory road, siren blaring, it sure as hell didn't help matters when Marge was back on the radio, excitedly notifying him that they were on state-wide, morning-television newscasts from both Metro Des Moines and the Quad Cities.

Lunch pails in hand, the factory's morning shift was arriving, Not a whole lot of time card punching-in was taking place. Most of the workers remained by their cars and pick-ups, fascinated with the drama taking shape.

Coming to grips with the situation, Rolli corralled Officer Wayne Emerson and Heartland plant exec Paul Weber. The three of them, shoulder to shoulder, began advancing on the tree grove. The Chief's bullhorn proved dispensable baggage. As they neared the park, Zeb Story was marching out to meet them.

Rolli wasted no time. "Who's in there, son?"

"Top of the morning to you too, Chief. Looks like a warm one."

Rolli was in no mood. "Cut the crap, Story. I want to know who and why."

Zeb had a list. "We've got Ana Story, Madison Weber, Autumn Hook, Lily Starr, and two Bradburys: Rachel and Jessica. All Troop 822. All fine."

"And?" Rolli stayed suspicious.

"The usual hoodlums from the Dry Dogs." Zeb tried to keep their exchange lighthearted. He didn't want to get Rolli started. "We all showed up to stop Lonnie and his boys from cutting down the oaks." Zeb smiled. "You're looking at a tree hugger, Chief."

"Is that what this is all about?" Confounded, Rolli challenged his fellow officer, "Know anything about this, Emerson?"

Wayne shook his head.

Rolli fumed with disgust. How had they fumbled the ball on this? He eyed Paul Weber. Knowing full well Madison was his daughter, he asked, sarcasm oozing, "Is that young Scout in there a relation of yours?"

Paul had a look, part revelatory part lost in Space.

Zeb intervened. "Our group is set to present terms for ending the standoff. We're low on water. We all need to wrap this up and have the Scouts back home, back at school, or in the case of Ana Story, back under house arrest forever. There's no cause for alarm here."

Rolli caught Zeb's drift and looked amused. "Confusion all around, eh Story?"

Zeb nodded and glanced at Paul Weber, one exasperated father to another.

"Your caper's being televised, Story," Rolli said, pointing at the KBOX van. "The whole goddamn state is watching."

Zeb was startled. "Horseshit."

"Hell no. The Department's getting calls. Concerned parents are on their way." Rolli provided Zeb a Cheshire grin. "Some might be carrying pitchforks."

"Give us fifteen minutes, Chief."

"I'm uniformed and uninformed, Story. I've no longer the patience to provide anyone with anything."

"These trees are over one hundred years old, Chief. Allow us ten minutes to present a case."

The morning breeze stiffened, noticeably colder, blowing harder from the north. Rolli, never taking his eyes off Zeb, hollered to an officer standing back up the hill by the patrol cars. "What's the latest radar, Marvin?"

"Tornado watch in effect 'til noon. Storms in the southwest. Might be headin' our way, Chief."

Rolli checked his watch and thought, With this wind picking up, maybe the bad weather will slide by to the south. He bore down on the biker. "Everyone a-ok in there?"

"Shifter's down. Bruised ribs. Maybe worse. Wants to stick it out. Scouts are good."

Rolli decided. His tone crackled with tension. "You're on the clock, Story. Eight minutes and counting. Any sign of a storm...get them all outta there. Are we God-Almighty clear on this?"

"Affirmative, sir." Zeb spun on his boot heels and jogged back to the grove. He heard the wrath in Chief Guy's voice trailing behind him. "...I'm all ears, Weber. You and Shimmer have got less than ten to explain this mess."

18
THE PACT

"You got seven minutes to get back out there with your Magna Carta, Hamilton."

"Now there's charity for ya. Seven's okay. We're near done here. Nice play, Captain."

While Zeb was buying time with the cops, the Alliance had meshed together ideas to win the day. Will Ribbs proposed a last minute add-on. "Let's include a line or two about filing state-required environmental impact reports." And the Weber girl was game. "Yeah, suppose we're standing on sacred Indian burial ground. Disturb the bones and Sugar City's cursed forever!"

"Good point," I admitted, "but let's not push Heartland up against a wall they can't climb. Right now we need a few simple ideas that can be agreed upon right away. I believe we got 'em. What do you say, Zeb? You're on a roll. Ready to present our pact?"

"I bought you a few minutes, Alex. As designated commander, it's your job to be emissary. And make it quick.

The chief's holding a short leash and Harlin needs looked after."

"No! *Wait!*"

All eyes fixed on wee Lily Starr.

"I suggest the biggest and strongest go out there and present our demands. We've got to show them we mean business." She pointed at Gordon Estey. "That guy's the one for sure."

Miss Starr's recommendation was heartfelt and her reasoning sound, but Gordon was not our best representative for reasons best left unsaid.

Fat chance.

Estey appeared spooked by Lily's proposal.

Propping himself up and groaning from the effort, Shifter added insult to injury. "What's your name, missy?"

"Lily Starr," she asserted, her voice carrying a hint of defiance.

"Well, Stardust, your scheme won't float 'cause the lummox can't read."

I tossed imaginary daggers at Shifter. This was hardly the time or place. We were all in this escapade together. The Blues were aware, to some extent, of Estey's limitations, but damn, why go public. Shifter's response was a coarse act of humiliation. Estey said not a word. The rest of us fidgeted uneasily, eager to move on. Our seven-minute window was closing fast. I was set to venture forth and offer up the Jackass Alliance Pact to Police Chief Guy—and said so.

Miss Starr saw no cause to retreat.

As a thirty-year-old single male, I am unfit to perceive the working mind of a newly minted female teenager. Given Shifter's revelation, I'd have bet that Lily's reaction would have been laced with discomfort, perhaps kicking herself for having spoken up at all and outing Estey's plight. I was dead-ass wrong. She marched directly over to him, looked straight up, like Samson to Goliath, and asked, "Is it true? You really can't read?"

The big guy recoiled, searching for a bulldozer to run him over and end this tortured confrontation. He stammered, "I...I...can read some."

She didn't buy it. "You're like a big empty warehouse, Mr. Estey."

All of us were taken aback by the encounter. Only Weber showed little surprise. After all, she herself had been one of Lily's classroom rehab projects. The Brainosaur was mission-minded, that's for sure.

Like lots of kids, I guess, Lily equated big with better. Huge guy Gordon Estey had to be hugely adept at all things, reading included. Gordon was a good-natured, stand-up guy. He'd be the first to admit to being a numbskull when it came to letters. At his age, he was probably too embarrassed to seek help, and who and where might he turn to anyway? The whole reading bane sat festering, akin to an overbearing relative you pray doesn't show up for the holidays. Now suddenly here *she* was, in the unlikeliest of places.

And Miss Starr wasn't providing much sympathy. "That why they call you Dimmer?"

I aimed to end the confrontation. I noticed, too, that the rest of the Scouts appeared bewildered at Lily's inquisition. At the last second, though, I held back. Even today, I'm unsure why. Watching poor Gordon shrug his massive shoulders, unable to respond, I felt his consternation and misery, but there are times, I suppose, when we all have to face the charging bull without the red cape.

Probing still, Lily asked, "Can you manage a few words?"

Gordon nodded. "Sure."

She held his stare a moment, decided, and confronted the group. "Mr. Estey and I will venture out and read the pact together."

And that is exactly what happened.

The two of them took our hastily drawn up document to the edge of the grove. There, they held a dry-run, slowly sizing up the provisions word for word. Zeb, sensing a problem, scrambled around and found an old saw cut log seat, lugging it to the two of them. With Lily atop the oak prop, she and Estey would stand near shoulder to shoulder. Ready-set-go, they marched off into the sunlight.

Olin Spoon told me later it was quite a sight watching the two of them emerge from the grove to face what had become a crowded hillside: Gordon, with his massive arms wrapped around a huge log, and Lily, lurching forward, matching his gait stride for stride. Word passes quickly in a small town. Some had caught the television newscast, others had access to police scanners, phones, e-mails, and text messaging. Lily's folks were there. Anxiety consumed them, and they could scarcely fathom their wee, shy academic partnering up with the oncoming leather giant. The crowd exchanged glances in total bewilderment.

Gordon and Lily found a level spot. He put the stump down. She stepped on up. As they were getting set, KBOX reporter Kelly Bauer saw her chance. Duck taping a wireless microphone to a light-stand, Kelly hustled down to them, positioning her makeshift assemblage directly in front. The two nervous envoys barely noticed her and the cameraman hovering nearby.

Onlookers crowded closer. The biker and the Scout stood facing Chief Guy and Heartland exec Paul Weber under a cooling sun that was giving way to a darkening western sky.

Sequestered among the oaks, Shifter insisted on a better vantage point. With everyone lending a hand, we relocated wounded warrior and picnic table together. Our entire Alliance was with him at the edge of the grove to see and hear the final act play out. I remember standing there—that very moment—thinking how glad I was to have seen this through.

WILDNUT PARK PACT

MAY 11, 2001

PROVISIONS

1. Immediate moratorium on removing trees from Wildnut Park

2. Emergency meeting be held by the Hardcastle County Board of Supervisors and the Sugar City (City) Council to determine ownership and fate of Wildnut Park. Alternative road construction plans for the industrial sector be submitted and reviewed. Assisting parties shall include the City Planning and Zoning Commission, the County Development Corporation, and all concerned citizens. The more the merrier.

3. As soon as possible—a referendum be held to protect Wildnut Park in perpetuity.

JACKASS ALLIANCE

We were too far removed to overhear clearly. Gordon
began well, booming out that everyone in the tree grove had
banded together as the Jackass Alliance and—"Here are our
terms."

He gave an anticipated, slow, staggered, halting, but
determined performance. We kept our fingers crossed
and occasionally winced as he stutter-stepped along. Lily
was fixated, there with him all the way, clearly and quietly
pronouncing those words causing Gordon to stumble. He'd
never command center stage, but I was proud of him as he
concluded, turning *perpetuity* into scrambled eggs. His
first try, *purr pet i tee*—not good, but Miss Starr set him
straight.

Most of those listening on the hillside remembered
Gordon Estey as the great football linesman. What they were
witnessing now was not a pretty site.

I saw Lily happily clap her hands as Gordon stepped
forward and presented the pact to Rolli Guy. The police chief
didn't waste a moment. This confrontation had gone on long
enough. In a loud voice, he exclaimed, "Sounds okay to me.
What does Heartland say, Mr. Weber? Can you live
with it?"

Paul, fully aware of the stiffening breeze and darkening
horizon, seconded quickly, "All provisions appear fair and
equitable. We accept the Alliance Pact. Let the town decide."

Rolli nodded and yelled at Gordon, "That's it, son. Now go and chase everyone out of that park," pointing to the western sky, "You've got *one* minute!!"

The stratosphere: at such heights, the updraft surge cools dramatically, creating a cauldron of ice crystals that rapidly diverge outward, flattening the dome of the towering cumulonimbus. Unfurling across the Midwest sky as if an iron anvil, the colossus, ten miles high, veers north at 50 mph. Swiftly falling high density frigid precipitation gives birth to a micro-downburst. The downdraft of violent wind and moisture explodes at the earth's surface.

19
THE TEMPEST

Our two go-betweens rushed back. Gordon looked ashen.
Quite the ordeal wee Lil had put him through. With an
embarrassed look-a-way, he accepted high fives and congrats.
From our vantage point at the edge of the grove, we had a
good enough view of the black southwestern sky. I sensed we
were okay, that we still had time as we commenced scrambling
about collecting our stuff. I shouted at Jessi and Zeb to lead
the Scouts out first. We'd follow on the bikes. Harlin insisted
he'd stagger out on his own. I was in doubt but let him slide
for the moment. We were all moving with a purpose, mere
minutes from shelter, from reaping a small victory.

So near.

Too late. Like a vampire's billowing black cape, the
tempest closed and engulfed us.

Folks gathered on the hillside recall first and foremost
how swiftly the towering storm stretched overhead, shrouding
sun and sky. No one saw a twister, but all watched in terror as
the monstrous anvil cloud emerged right before their eyes;

resulting in a mad dash to safety within the solid confines of Heartland Ironworks.

As for myself, I often relive the suddenness of the storm's onslaught. So overwhelmed at the unexpected fury, not a bone joint would bend. I stood as rigid and rooted as the giant oaks surrounding me.

A howling, hurricane-force wind tore through the grove. Everything and everyone not nailed down or holding on with a death grip was tossed like tumbleweed. There came a splintering, ripping roar. The earth shook beneath our feet. My eyes were riveted on the sentinel, the towering great white that stood guard at the north side of the park; the oak that Harlin and Zeb had raced to protect, the one to my recollected horror, that had already felt the sting of the chainsaws bite. In disbelief I watched the old sentinel violently wrenched from its mooring and hurled skyward.

Silhouetted against the enclosing darkness, the tree was defying gravity; twisting, near-somersaulting in the gale. A dizzying array of lightning strikes, resembling a thousand flickering phosphorescent bulbs, provided a morbidly fascinating psychedelic backdrop. The huge oak was a string puppet, made to do jumping-jacks in the sky by a mad puppeteer.

Then, directly overhead, caught in a downdraft, the tree plunged earthward. Seconds before the calamity, someone, I believe Robin, screamed, "Run! Oh God, run!" Everyone took flight. All but one. Shock held me in place. Honing in like a ballistic missile, the tree was spearing down upon our lives too quickly. I witnessed out of the corner of my eye three of the Scouts holding hands, running toward the hillside. But Lily, Autumn, and Rachel had no chance of escaping the missiles flight path. Veering in on the three like a huge jackrabbit, Gordon's wide wingspan encircled them from behind, the four falling face-first to the ground. Further right, I glimpsed Jessi sprinting at her daughter. She had the same protective fixation as Gordon, but had too much ground to cover. At the last instant before the tree hit, Zeb, racing, reached her, grabbed her waist from behind, then pirouetted around like an Olympic shot putter, throwing her with all his strength toward safer ground.

That was all I saw as the sentinel fell from the sky; a destructive totem heaven sent and hell bent.

My ears were attuned to sound: branches cracking and breaking, frightened human cries, the scream of the howling wind, an unearthly shrill. I expected to be crushed. Surely I, the proprietor of the circumstance, stood as designate ground zero. I suppose my last thought on this mortal coil was quite simple: how can a tree be falling on my head?

Robin, Ribbs, and Shifter were together as the tragedy unfolded. Shifter draped his arms around their shoulders. They lifted him at the knee and quickstepped westward. By pure chance, they were moving in the right direction.

Madison and Ana ran south, but tripped and fell from the wind's fury. In that final moment before the falling trees' impact, Madison looked up and rolled to cover and protect her fellow Scout.

THE RESPONDERS

Tess Pepper punched memory 2 speed-dial and crossed her fingers. Bobbi Brinkerhoff picked up on the first ring. "Hey, Bank Shot, you surviving?"

"God, Tess, we're hunkered down in the old root-cellar with the cobwebs and the spiders. Remind me to clean out this dungeon one day, will ya? We're okay, just praying the homestead hasn't spun off to Kansas. Criminy, Tess, that was the blackest, ugliest storm cloud I ever wanna see."

"Ditto. Take a peak outside, Brink. Dispatch called. Chief Guy wants the entire EMS Team to muster ASAP."

"My pager's squawking as we speak. What's going on?"

"Don't rightly know yet. Yer cloud unloaded. Maybe a twister. Folks out at Wildnut Park near the ironworks factory are hurt. Chief sounded close to panic, and sister, Rolli just don't get panic. Know what I'm saying? So hoof it."

"Billi's here. Home on break before finals."

"We'll make it a Redhawk Scream Team reunion. Meet at the firehouse. Double-time it, Bank Shot. You two are late already!"

In a death spiral, the old sentinel oak roared down from the sky, ripping through the tree grove, a thousand limbs cracking and snapping. As if the tree's fall was meant as a final curtain, the howling wind blast abated. In the aftermath of the impact with Mother Earth, an eerie quiet ensued. Leaves and dust particles danced gently about in ballet-like serenity.

Thick oak branches trapped me on all sides, but for an inexplicable reason I remained upright and unscathed. Behind and to my right, unmistakable teenage screams pierced the semi-darkness. As my eyesight slowly adjusted to the storm's foggy gray, I scrambled frantically to free myself from the clawing, gnarly tentacles.

With a frightening crack of thunder, the cries of those hurt were swiftly smothered by torrential rain, as hard a deluge as imaginable. This tempest from Hades was arriving in stages each as devastating as the one before. Using my drenched leather jacket for head cover, I began to stumble half-blindly toward the cries for help.

Gordon Estey was sprawled face down and half-rational, having been struck hard in the head and pinned tight by a falling tree limb. The weight on his spine was massive. Shooting pain and the stinging hard rain kept him semi-aware, preventing a slip into unconsciousness. Beside him, Autumn's anguished cries hushed to a whimper. The cold drenching was adding to her misery. Delirium was taking hold, a trauma more frightening to Estey than her screams that came before.

But Lily was the one who commanded his attention. Their two faces close together, he heard her barely audible whisper, "Mr. Estey...can't breathe...suffocating." Her eyes began to flutter. Having ensnared the three Scouts on the run, trapping them, he *had* to do something. Shouting Lily's name in a panic, he saw her eyes reopen. He managed to turn his head. Rachel had her back to him, lying still. He nudged her once, twice, pleading, "You all right? Can you hear me?" Back came a frightened reply, "I...I guess."

"Okay. Listen up now." He spoke slowly and gently, attempting to masquerade his fear. "I'm going to try and raise up. When I do, get out from under, then both of you pull the other girl free. I think she's hurt pretty bad. Ready?" Rachel and Lily mouthed two trembling okays. "Good. We can do this. Move fast. On three. Here we go. One...two..."

Gordon Estey might have called on the fortitude of his ancestors or rendered the will of God, but it was the plea from Lily that propelled him. The resignation in her cry *can't breathe*, his anger and terror that those words might be her last, drove him to find strength he'd never known. Struggling to position his arms, *"Three!"* He pushed.

The strain was unbearable, but almost as a dream his chest rose allowing two young Scouts to scramble out from underneath. Over the din from the downpour, he heard the girls struggling.

"Grab her and pull."

"Her leg's caught."

"Slide her this way, Lily. Can you push that branch away? We need space."

"I'm trying. Not much help, Rach. I feel faint. Oh God! Auti!"

"Stay with her, Lily. I'll go for help."

Mere seconds. That was all he held on for. Estey's arms turned rubbery and collapsed. The pain overwhelmed. He lay unconscious.

Buried under a small mountain of foliage, Madison and Ana fought like cats to free themselves. Luckily, they'd been struck by the tree's top, thinner branches. The hard rain began to lessen. The sky was brightening as the scattered, broken storm passed on to the northeast.

Climbing through a maze, the two girls physically vaulted over, ducked under, and broke limbs before finally escaping their prison. Ana glanced at her fellow troop with relief—and screamed. Madison's face was covered in blood.

Madison recoiled, alarmed but uncertain. She didn't feel a thing.

Ana screamed again, "Maddy! Don't touch!" She got close, trying to find cuts. It was too dark.

Rain was falling. Blood seeped into Madison's eyes, blinding her. Confusion turned to panic. "Ana!"

"I'm right here." Ana grasped her hand. "Don't let go. Come on, we'll find the others."

"Ana, my ankle's twisted and starting to hurt a ton."

"Lean on me, *amiga*. Keep the weight off." She wrapped her arm around Madison's waist. "We can do this." Ana tasted bile rising in her throat. "Ay, Maddy. Your face. Your beautiful face."

Entwined, the two hobbled off; Rachel's not-too-distant shouts for help willed them onward.

Dazed. Still standing. I administered a 360-degree physical, my hands roaming over and around my body. Arms and legs were still attached. I hadn't a freaking scratch on me. Layer upon layer of huge oak branches entombed me, but nary a one crushed or mangled, not even a caress. I was ground-zero. How? Why?

"*Hamilton!* That you? You okay in there?"

The hammering rain was slackening. I recognized Ribbs's voice and pinpointed his silhouette in the receding darkness, Robin too, thank God. "I'm still in one piece. Just need to climb out from under. Go on. Find Rachel. I'll follow."

"*Mercy!*" That was all Robin managed to muster as Ana and Madison found us. Appearing in the mist like two shell-shocked haunted survivors from Gettysburg, they were mud-spattered, drenched, and listlessly draped arm-in-arm. Madison was dragging a lame foot, blood streaming down her face, blood everywhere, an incomprehensible scene.

Triage began with the wounded soldier.

She objected. "I'm okay. Let me help,"

We screamed , "NO!" and forced her to lay down, head up, leg up. We ripped shirts for compress. Ribbs, cleaning Madison's face and scalp found no deep cuts, and wrapped her mummy-like, all the while guiding us through a broken branch tied ankle brace.

Demanding Madison to lie still, we gathered around the stricken. Autumn, clammy and shaking, had slipped into shock. Lily was pale and hyperventilating. Gordon lay trapped and unresponsive. All of us together failed to budge the limb atop him. We were able to free Autumn completely. Her lower left leg had been crushed. The severity of the injury sent shivers, but it was Lily, eyes seemingly rolled back into her head, gasping for breath, that scared the shit out of me. Ribbs made sure she wasn't choking. Tapping her chest, he suspected a collapsed lung.

There can't be a more unnerving sight than witnessing a living creature struggle for air. The anxiety is unbearable. Lily's wind pipe appeared to sag off to one side. Ribbs sat transfixed over the stricken girl. I watched him nod his head as if arriving at a hard-fought decision. He cried out to me, "Hamilton! I could lose her. We need...*what*?! Think, sawbones. Dammit. *Think!*" Will was pounding his head with the palm of his hand. "Alex, *the bikes!* Get me a piece of brake line. Six inches. Cut it. Snap it off. I don't care how you do it. You've got thirty seconds. We're near fatal here. Go! *go!*"

Darting off, I heard our doc shout, "I need a rubber glove, people. Find me a glove!" I tore for the cycles, weaving my way about and around the fallen tree, located my Harley crushed under a heap of limbs, and assaulted the brake-line with my bare hands.

Getting back, near out of breath, everyone was assisting Autumn. I shouted and held up my prize. Ribbs grabbed for it, eyeing the hollow shiv as a heaven-sent gift. He stuck it in his mouth and blew, clearing fluid, then taped a torn off rubber glove finger at one end. The two of us scrambled to Lily's side.

She was turning blue. Ribbs had positioned Madison to hold her close. She was cradling Lily's head in her lap, all the while rambling on softly about future plans and together adventures yet to come.

I knelt transfixed, as Ribbs felt for a spot down from Lily's armpit, scanned quickly skyward asking for Divine guidance, then, pushing hard, plunged the razor-sharp brake line into Lily's chest. She screamed in agony. Madison, her face still haphazardly wrapped in bloody gauze, kept on with her one-way conversation, whispering, not missing a beat. Forced air from Lily's chest cavity exploded up through our motorcycle catheter, flapping the makeshift rubber valve. Ribbs was visibly shaken as he instructed Madison to hold the shiv in place, to keep her comforted. He shook himself free and rushed back to Autumn.

We'd torn anything left available to shreds for tourniquet and compress. Will's hands flew to stem the bleeding. He recognized a leg artery was severed and knew the blood loss would kill Autumn in minutes.

Despite William Ribbs's steady concentration, the dire situation in the tree grove set off a flashback: Vietnam, the Central Highlands, 2nd Platoon Bravo Company pinned down by sniper fire and incoming mortar rounds; explosions, screams, the rush to save the wounded. Like then, as now, there was not a moment to spare.

Attending Autumn, playing mental telepathic games with Gordon, keeping a wary eye on Lily, Will silently beseeched the three of them to fight for life. Hold on. No postmortems allowed. Unthinkable. Dammit, hold on.

I sat and closed my eyes. Surely the madness surrounding me was not happening. Surely I'm home asleep, tossing and turning, having a nightmare. Any second now I'll shake awake and realize this is all a bad dream. My eyes opened. I prayed for four walls and a ceiling, but all I saw were waves of dancing light. I'd forgotten. We'd never been completely alone. Flashlights! Help was arriving from every direction.

Harlin Shifter lay alone, resting on his backside, breathing quietly. Any quick movement shot paralyzing abdominal pain. Eyes shut, he tried to block further misery from the cold rain by listening to the voices off in the distance. He made out Ribbs barking instructions. From the tone and temperament, he knew whatever was happening or had happened, wasn't good. He felt an uneasiness. Images behind his eyes flickered then vanished. Who? Where? A puzzle piece was missing. His heart beat quicker. Evil was stalking the timber, gaining advantage in the confusion, grinning from a horror overlooked. Shifter's fear was growing. Suddenly he had a clear vision; a fright. Where was Zeb? The one voice he hadn't heard. The one voice he should be hearing, taking charge, supporting Ribbs. Shaking, he thought back as the storm hit and the tree fell, a recorded vision of Zeb racing hard at Jessi. They were south of him, not far. Without thinking, Harlin rolled sideways. Pain brought forth a gasp. Slower now, he positioned himself. Walking was no longer possible, but supporting himself on all fours kept the shooting stabs at bay. He could crawl.

Believing he'd have to navigate over the massive, toppled tree trunk, Shifter gave himself little chance starting out. The grove and the sky were still dark from the storm; he was crawling blind. Minutes passed that felt like hours as he urged himself forward, under and over limbs, squinting through rain, and praying for more light. Lady Luck was walking point. He caught a glimpse of Zeb's boots extending from a mountain of branches. Shouts brought no response. Hurrying, absorbing pain from his crushed ribs, he maneuvered close. His heart froze. Zeb was unconscious lying face down in water. He'd been struck, knocked senseless, and had collapsed in a ground depression. The torrential rain that followed created a drowning pool.

Mustering his waning strength, Shifter was able to reach and turn Zeb face up. The deadly branch had split apart on impact. He was not trapped, and Harlin pulled enough to slide Zeb's head and shoulders to higher ground. The effort exhausted him. Arching Zeb's neck and pinching his nose, he went mouth-to-mouth, forcing air into Zeb's lungs, all in vain. His own condition prevented resuscitation. He hadn't the breath. Frantic and enraged over his own uselessness, Shifter spied all directions. Where the hell was Jessi? She *had* to be nearby. He hollered out with all that his body allowed. Close at hand but hidden by a decline, she heard him. "I'm trapped."

"Well ya better free yourself, Bradbury. Yer boyfriend up here got his self near-dead and drowned, and I'm as useless as peeing on a prairie fire."

Jessi didn't need to hear another word. With a frantic effort she scratched, clawed, even bit herself free. Putting weight on her right side made her cry out. She remembered running hard at Rachel as the tree fell. Then, the sensation of being grabbed from behind and tossed sailing through the air, believing herself caught in a tornado and that she would surely die—then crashing hard on her shoulder and hearing the bone snap. Now able to elbow crawl, grasping limbs with one hand for support, she hauled her way up the slope. Cresting the ridge she spotted the two of them. Harlin was rocking back and forth, cradling Zeb. Fighting back panic, she screamed for help.

The storm was abating. She was heard.

"That's my mom!"

"Rachel, we're making headway here. Go find her. Do what you can," Ribbs directed. "You stay, Ana. I need you with me." Whatever had gone wrong with Zeb, Will didn't want his daughter at the scene.

Shifter exhaled a sigh of relief at seeing Jessi. Maybe Zeb had a fighting chance. "Glad you joined the party, Bradbury. He's not breathing. I'll brace his neck. You're the kisser. Five quick breaths. Give them some heat."

Scrambling close, Jessi mumbled a quick prayer, locked on Zeb's lips, and transferred the gift of life.

He lay still. No movement.

"It's not working, Harlin! I can't find a pulse. Oh God!"

"Keep trying."

"Mom! Mom!"

Rachel's calls, nearby, diverted Jessi's attention. "Over here, Rach," she shouted back. "Go get help! We need help here."

Rachel stumbled upon them. "I'm not going anywhere for help. I'm bringing it."

Harlin and Jessi held looks of recognition and deliverance as Rachel appeared with Billi and Bobbi Brinkerhoff trailing right behind.

Jess cried out, *"He's not breathing!"*

"Found him lying face down in water," Shifter blurted, eyeing the sisters as heavenly angels. "If it ain't the Brink twins. You are a beautiful sight. Prettiest gals west of the Mississip."

Billi Brinkerhoff pointed at Shifter. "Forget about this one, sis, he's totally delirious." The two First Responders began CPR. Donning a pocket mask, Billi administered two deep breaths. She probed Zeb's neck for a pulse. Nothing.

Rachel and Jessi knelt together, arms wrapped around one another, waiting, watching for signs of life. The tension grew unbearable.

Billi tried to lessen the fear and dread that surrounded them. "Gimme more pressure on his sternum, Bobbi. Unlike Shifter, this one's worth saving."

Harlin reciprocated. "Now Billi, just cause I once planted a long ago kiss and whispered your sister's name, is no reason to bury a man before his time."

Humor failed. Not now. Not today.

Bobbi stayed stoic. Concentrating, straddling Zeb, applying pressure with the heel of her hands, she counted off thirty repetitions, whispering, "Come on. Come on."

Under a rumbling sky, amidst the echoing voices of rescuers nearby, the five: Shifter, two Brinkerhoffs and two Bradburys, rhythmically labored and silently prayed as if cocooned and oblivious to all around them.

Jessi arched her neck, praying skyward. Shifter lay alongside Zeb, reduced now to a spectator's role. Rachel sat, near-comatose, tears creeping across a grimy, gaunt thirteen-year-old face that had already seen too much. The Brinkerhoffs urged each other on. Bobbi fought down panic. They were losing him. "Billi! Let's send Jessi for the AED. This guy needs a jolt."

"Can't risk it, sis. He's soaked and we're all sitting in water. Keep your rhythm. All right now, here we go with a three point winner. One more time." Billi forced in two deep breaths of air.

Tension gave way to hysteria. Jessi and Rachel simultaneously bent down close to Zeb's face and screamed, "BREATHE!!"

Incredibly, the sun found a clearing amongst the dark clouds. Rays of light cascaded down through the oaks. A gentle rain continued to fall and Jessi witnessed ribbons of rainbow colors dancing in the grove, as Zeb suddenly heaved, jerked sideways, and vomited breakfast and muddy water all over Harlin Shifter.

Harlin gagged and spit. With a sour chuckle, and the resignation of the truly weary, he offered up a summation to no one in particular. "Ahhhhh, thus ends this splendid morn'."

20
THE NEWS CREW

Positioning stanchions and blockers, Joey Rockland
found the lighting to his satisfaction. Everything this morning
had been ad-libbed. At last, time allowed for a staged shot.
Reporters teased him about being anal over his set-up
routine. That was expected. He just wanted the exposure
right, especially this one. "Ready, Kelly?" Double checking his
backdrop, "Got an opening?"

Kelly nodded, apprehensive.

"Wait. You look like a drowned rat. Roberto! Makeup! We
could use some help here."

"Stuff it, Joey. I ain't walkin' down the aisle. Let's do this."

"Hey, Bauer. Chill. I'm kidding. *Capisce?*"

Holding a microphone, Kelly exhaled a weary smile.
Earlier, as the storm abated and swept eastward, the three
abandoned camera and cable and had sprinted into the grove
to aid the Emergency Medical Team. Tending to those hurt,
lending a hand with stretcher duty, they chipped in their best
to assist the kids to the county hospital as fast as possible. Kelly

was drifting, recalling the overwhelming wind and rain, *that tree,* and the frenzied rescue.

"Kelly? Earth to Kelly."

"Huh? Don't look at me like that, Rockland. I'm fine."

"Pull it all together, Bauer. No small potatoes here. Roberto has us hooked up. We're juiced to go live. No tapes. No mistakes. The whole world is watching." Joey smiled encouragement. "Watch me, Kelly. Stay natural. You'll be aces."

From the van, Roberto gave the signal.

"Now, KB. Be a pro. We're rolling."

"...the last ambulance has left. Everyone at this juncture is alive. As witnessed firsthand, injuries were severe, but again no deaths have been reported. The scene of the devastation, here at Wildnut Park outside Sugar City, is nearly deserted now. I'm speaking to you under a clear blue sky. Hard to imagine a deadly thundercloud swept through less than one hour ago. How quickly it struck. How quickly it dissipated. It's now..." without thinking, Kelly looked at her watch "...9:20 in the morning but it's already been a very long day in this small, southeastern Iowa town. With cameraman Joey Rockland and engineer Roberto Arandas, this is Kelly Bauer...an exhausted Kelly Bauer... returning you to the KBOX Studio."

———————

Assignment Editor Joan Chase and News Director George Ridgefield were reviewing Kelly Bauer's final images from Sugar City. George sighed, "She might have concluded without the *exhausted* sign-off. Touch of grandstanding there."

"I don't think so. More a knee-jerk rendering. I don't see or hear any premeditation," Joan reflected. "Our Ms. Bauer has captured something here. Her entire report reveals the strain, even her obvious inexperience works for her. Unorthodox perhaps, but there's an immediacy that shines. She's struck a nerve."

Ridgefield nodded. "With viewers, that's for certain. Anyone flipping channels this morning stayed with us. The numbers will be through the roof." He let out a half-laugh. "Crazy business. I apologize, Joan. I was wrong yesterday to dismiss this. You made a good call. Who *was* our voice-of-reason character anyway?"

"Still don't know," Joan nearly laughed, "and hardly a great call. The whole circumstance with our gal being on-the-spot was a fluke. We'll need follow-up. The Bauer crew is at the hospital as we speak. We need names, and it's crucial we find someone to explain to our viewers just what the hell went on out there this morning. Bauer's early-on purporting Girl Scout kidnappers woke up the entire state. A critical overreach on her part for sure. Regardless, her story may have legs."

"Legs?" George Ridgefield had the look of a scatback who'd taken a handoff with nothing but daylight in front of him. "My God, Joan, this story's got Louisa May Alcott and the Hell's Angels being tossed about in a Shakespearean tempest. The story doesn't have legs, it's got stilts!"

Joan squinted a skeptical eye. "Aside from all that, I'm betting the attorney general has Sugar City on his front-burner.

Let's get our capitol crew out knocking on doors over at AG, see what shakes out."

"Has there been a wilder Seven in memory?"

Joan patted him on the back. "Not on my watch."

"You realize, Joan, don't you, that Rockland may be looking at The National Press Award; capturing that tree being ripped aloof and sent hurtling into the park. Monty and the weather techs are examining Joey's film like a treasure map. The kid hung in there. Recorded it all. Unbelievable. Our crazy storm-chaser cameraman got all he wished for and then some."

"Some of those kids were seriously injured, George. I'm certain Joey's got more on his mind than recognition."

He was only half-listening. "But you know, Joan, it isn't the storm video that mesmerizes. No sir." The news director raised a finger to emphasize his point. "It was those two first walking out then standing side-by-side. The hulking biker dude stumbling through...what did they call it?"

She remembered clearly. "The Jackass Alliance Pact."

"Yeah, right." He snapped his fingers. "The whole Mutt-and-Jeff routine. Talk about priceless."

She stood silent as Ridgefield kept on.

"I'll tell you another thing. I was there in the newsroom. Every scribe was glued to the monitors and *no* one was laughing at that biker, not a snicker. Nelson Hitch was there. You know what he says, out loud, at the end of Bauer's telecast?"

Joan waited.

"Hitch, our resident linguistic overseer, stands up and I quote: Don't sweat it, kid. No one can properly pronounce *perpetuity*. Damn, Joan! It was as if the lummox represented some sort of Everyman. Seeing him struggle was like living through our own worst fears: there, but for the grace of God, go I. Am I making any sense?"

"Christ-like."

"Absolutely." George appeared uncomfortable. "We never had this conversation, Ms. Chase."

Joan laughed. "I've not known your philosophical side, Mr. Ridgefield. I like it. And remind me, George, when I finally catch up with our Ms. Bauer, to simply start yelling. Going off on her own. That girl is in so much trouble. I'll have her on beat-call for months."

Ridgefield gave a slight harrumph. "Yes...well...amidst all the hostilities don't forget to tell those kids they did a great job." His face radiated merriment. "Didn't a certain assignment editor go on the other day about how we were all young once?"

"Touché, your directorship. I still want to know how she conned two experienced techs into her scheme."

"Seems to me I read years ago how a pretty face once launched a thousand ships."

Joan smiled. The two of them continued to watch intently as the early morning telecast replayed. "Fascinating," Joan noted, "how the camera falls in love with one face while dismissing so many others." She was forced to admit. Kelly

Bauer had it. Whatever *it* was. "She'll be our lead at Six and Ten?"

George Ridgefield acknowledged, "Unless the world ignites in conflagration; Sugar City's our lead tonight."

SATURDAY, MAY 12, 2001

21
THE CHIEF

"Yeah, what is it, Marvin?" Sugar City Police Chief Rolli Guy was annoyed. He'd instructed his office staff: No calls.

"Sorry, Chief. I've got John Katz from the county conservation board on his cell. Says it can't wait."

Rolli rolled his eyes. Since the storm Friday morning his office had been under siege with "urgent" and "can't wait." He manhandled the receiver. "Johnny?"

"I'm out at Wildnut. You need to ride out and have a look at this, Chief."

"What?"

"Just make the trip."

Rolli sighed, exasperated. "Maybe late afternoon. Right now I'm rehashing events with a rep from the attorney general's..."

"No time to lose. Bring him with you."

THREE DAYS LATER
TUESDAY, MAY 15, 2001

22
THE INQUEST

"Good afternoon to you all. My name's Chute. I'm
an attorney. A mostly retired judge," Cyrus scanned the
assembled, noting he had everyone's rapt attention, "residing
and practicing a tad up north in Liberty County. Some folks
there wish I'd quit permanently, but," exhaling an indulgent
chuckle, "like an old plow horse, I still enjoy, at times, mixing
with the herd." Chute stuck out his chin, expectant, but his
country banter was met with stony silence. The standing-room-
only crowd resembled a hospital waiting room full of anxious
family members and friends.

Not quite the time-worn plow horse, the judge was a robust
man with an expressive, cherubic face. He wore a faded, gray-
striped, seersucker suit, white dress shirt, white tie. He had
hair the color of straw, disheveled in a style best described
as grandfatherly slack. This guy might have arrived direct
from central casting: the hayseed shyster whose good-old-boy
theatrics belied a razor-sharp legal mind. Short and stout, he
emitted a healthy glow. One might catch a twinkle in his eye,
but Cyrus was not in Sugar City to hand out holiday gifts.

"And I'm here representing the attorney general of Iowa. Pertaining to the events surrounding May 11, I stand before you, at his request, for one purpose: to learn the truth."

"With me today is Ms. Effie Poole, also from the Liberty County seat, who will act as recorder. She and I have worked together since the Roosevelt Administration. If I become lost or tongue-tied, she'll be my rescue." Surveying the crowded room over his reading glasses, he noted, "No offense Ms. Poole, but I'd rather not say which Roosevelt."

"No offense taken," Effie responded. "We're as old as we feel."

The crowded room responded at last with some good-natured chuckling. Effie Poole was a tall, handsome woman with a quick smile. Teddy and Franklyn Roosevelt had harvested some sorely needed comic relief within the room.

Chute pressed on. "Unless we note beforehand, all we say here will go on permanent record. Now then...the truth," the judge repeated, "an ideal that seems in short supply these days." He looked down, rifling through papers scattered on the table. Finding what he was searching for, he asked, "A Miss Madison Weber, I wonder if you might define the word *truth* for all of us here today?"

Heads shifted. She looked like hell: on crutches supporting an ankle cast, two black eyes one worse than the other, a swollen lower lip stitched together, whiplash facial wounds all in varying healing modes—a veritable exhumed cadaver.

Singling her out, Judge Chute caught the fourteen-year-old girl off guard. Quickly she fortified herself—no tears. As one of the few in Troop 822 still upright, she willed herself to represent them with resolve. She had led them out there and had best stand for them now.

She'd cut her hair. Gone was the Prince Valiant look, the shoulder-length locks she'd carried from elementary classes. Her mom had been *so* against it, near heartbroken. Dad, natch, refused to take sides; chickenhearted, but probably wise. In the end, it was her head, her hair. "Mom! It'll grow. I *have* to do this." With the shearing, punk ruled. Short, jelled wisps jutted out at odd angles, all the more striking given her hairs natural jet-black hue. Adding in her healing scars and stitching, she barely recognized herself. A defiance reflected back from the mirror. Score one for the rebel.

"And if I might inquire," Chute found her, "how are you feeling today?"

"Okay, I guess. I feel better than I look." Madison got right to the point. "I'd say, your honor, that the truth is pretty much like a greased pig. Hard to get a handle on."

I smiled along with a lot of folk. She was a dead-ringer for death warmed over, but still full of spunk.

Chute wavered. As he suspected, she was a playmaker, not to be taken lightly. "It's my hope, Miss Weber, that you and I can wrap our arms around this pig and keep a firm grip"

Madison simply nodded.

Chute returned his attention to the room at large. "My role here is that of a legal advisor to the attorney general; in layman's terms, an outside-the-fishbowl troubleshooter." He paused and reached for his glass of water; taking a few sips, collecting his thoughts. "The AG sought me out. 'Get yourself down to Sugar City,' he directed, 'and determine how in blazes it all came about. If there's liability involved, I need to know. If there's abduction or child endangerment involved, I want to know by whom. Should indictments be handed down, charges filed? I want recommendations, Cyrus. I don't want to see unwarranted civil suits and counter suits clogging up the system. I don't want that town torn apart more than Mother Nature already has. Meet with the folks and get to the bottom of this tragedy.'" Chute reached for the pitcher at hand and refilled his water glass. "And those are today's marching orders, good people." He took time for another drink. In doing so, he reflected back to his meeting with the AG. He and Maxwell Cox had known each other for decades and Cyrus was startled to see and hear his reserved, scholarly compatriot so unglued over this Sugar City affair.

"What the hell were the television cameras doing out there? KBOX, Des Moines? Hardly their local beat. The entire episode has been blown out of proportion, Cyrus. Sky high! Every wilderness federation and land trust is on my case. Dare I relate the earfuls received from Girl Scout National HQ? In a nutshell, everyone's clamoring, 'Why is the State of Iowa running roughshod over Girl Scouts in order to kill trees?' The mind reels, Cyrus. My office phone lines are worn thin attempting to transmit who, how, and why."

Cyrus had never witnessed the AG this animated.

"We're all over the Internet. Start with KBOX. I've been informed their server is down from excess traffic. Apparently their filmed segment has gone viral, uploaded and posted by weather service sites and hundreds of others. I'm talking national, Cyrus. The Sugar City affair is growing like a summer dandelion."

"It's a brand new interconnected world, Max."

"I do not wish to be interconnected. Motorcycle gangs, Cyrus. E-mailing. Wanting to lend a hand. Stand guard. An outfit calling themselves the Sky Wolves checked in from San Diego. San Diego, for heaven's sake, determined to show solidarity. Ready to, in their own words, 'saddle up.' Can you imagine? Jesus. Moreover, on top of the kids getting seriously hurt, we're facing a PR fiasco. Find a lid, Cyrus. Cap this thing before the State gets a black eye on *60 Minutes* or some such news show. Iowa's buzzing, Cyrus, and I'm in the dark. Not a good place. Get down there. Get some answers."

Now, launching his inquest, Chute was quite aware Iowa's top lawyer may have been overstating. Still, he was energized at being the veritable spear tip probing into a deep-well of public interest.

Windows were open wide in the commons room welcoming in a pleasant day offering up scattered clouds and a light northerly breeze. The storm had swept away the lingering humidity. Late spring coolness was in the air. Traffic on main was light to nonexistent. The quiet outside provided a sense that the town's natural flow of energy was all packed together under one roof in the commons room.

Chute grew more pointed. "For those directly involved...I'm not here to threaten or pamper. If you feel the need to offer excuses for actions taken. Fine. If you want to offer up a justified defense. Make your point. Here to apologize? Take your time. But if you elect to stonewall and/or deceive, then leave this minute. Door's right over there."

Not a soul moved.

"Now, people, as I'm sure you're all aware, you have the right as American citizens to seek counsel; to not answer questions; to not..." The judge appeared to lose his concentration.

"Self-incriminate." Effie Poole didn't even look up from her silent typing.

"Yes, to not implicate yourselves. Thank you, Effie." Chute paused, returning stares. "Or, as I recall my young nephew once saying over a broken window, 'I'm pitching the Fifth, Pappy.'"

Everyone, listening intently, contributed to a collective grin, as if we all suddenly remembered to breathe again.

"This forum is not a grand jury investigation," the judge informed. "No one has been subpoenaed. To those about to give testimony...remember there are family and friends attending today that have a fervent wish to comprehend the events this past Friday. They have a right to closure."

Chute took a seat, removed a handkerchief, and wiped his brow. I recognized he'd given a bravura opening and knew there was no holding back. The notes had been played days ago. I stood with fingers crossed that they'd been in tune.

Nearly everyone concerned had gathered at the community center; perhaps as unique a Sugar City congregation yet on record. Quite a few attending had their picture on the walls. Someone years ago had liberated old graduation pictorials gathering dust in the high school storage room, and hung them chronologically along the commons' walls. The senior class photos dated back to World War I, and I always got a kick reviewing the changing hairstyles as the twentieth century lived and passed on. For any budding salon hair stylist looking for new old-ideas, this was the place to visit.

The judge commanded a platform up front within the large square commons room. Every chair alongside six extended tables, normally used for receptions and senior meals, was filled. Many, myself included (too fidgety to sit), leaned against walls or perched on the south side window sills. Madison and a few others had commandeered high chairs from the kitchen. Heartland Iron had sent a corporate agent from Chicago. Movers and shakers included the town council and the sheriff's department. The remainder were involved commissions and county boards mingled in with lots of Sugar City folk with an interest. Why not? It was an open town meeting.

ROBIN

"I thought we might begin with a Ms. Robin Emerson."

Robin sat up straight, cupping her hands to her cheeks. She was shocked at hearing the judge raise her name. She simply figured her minor role, minuscule in fact, would be overlooked at the inquest. Why me? What in the world?

"Now, Ms. Emerson," Chute found her, his reading glasses perched precariously on the tip of his nose, "according to this police report, you were arrested last Friday morning by Officer Wayne Emerson. Relation of yours?"

"Husband, your honor."

"You were apprehended and processed by your husband?" The judge registered surprise

"Yes, sir."

Intervening, Police Chief Rolli Guy noted, "If you please, your honor. The word arrest might not properly convey the situation on the eleventh. Mrs. Emerson and Alexander Hamilton were the only two that emerged from the grove free of injury. They were both transported to town for questioning. Neither were formerly arrested or charged."

Chute sat silent a few seconds, then turned back to Robin. "Your being detained last Friday morning must make for interesting dinner conversation, Ms. Emerson."

Robin gave a quick, hard stare at Wayne across the room. "Or lack thereof, your honor."

The assembled fidgeted about with nervous laughter.

"Might I ask, Ms. Emerson, what brought you to the park that Friday?"

Robin cringed. She wasn't prepared to deal with this. Not here. Not now. But the judge left her little choice. "I'm with the club, your honor. A member of the Blues."

Surprised again, Chute queried, "You were with the motorcycle gang?"

"Yes, your honor, but club, not gang."

Cyrus shrugged. "How many members constitute this... this...Blues?"

"Seven, your honor."

"Other women?"

"No, sir."

"Forgive me, but I'm intrigued, Ms. Emerson. Exactly how long have you been a club member?"

Robin gazed around the room and saw the astonished faces of friends and family in attendance. Inwardly she felt a cathartic triumph; her secret life revealed: the mousy soccer-mom as hardcore Bonnie Biker. A complete sham of course, but not without a delicious connotation or two. "Six days your honor."

"Six days!" Chute's bushy eyebrows made a vertical leap. "Hardly enough time before leaping into the fire."

Robin was sure Zeb was about to join in the dialogue, but she was having none of that. Quickly, she said, "Zeb Story, our club's president, did not...in fact, your honor, none of the members pressed me take part last Friday. If I recall correctly, I volunteered. I *insisted* I play a role at Wildnut Park."

Chute remained inquisitive. "Why the determination?"

"Joining the motorcycle club was a big step for me. The whole process was difficult. After being voted in, having won their acceptance, brand new member or not, I wasn't going to remain behind the first time a line was drawn in the sand. The Blues elected to show up and help save the trees. I was riding with them."

The judge had ascertained enough. "Thank you, Ms. Emerson." He silently acknowledged this young woman while puzzling over the agitated husband, perhaps the fool. Robin Emerson had spirit.

JULE

Chute stood, arching his back. "Pardon, folks. Chiropractor's orders. If I sit too long a spell, my bones take on the tendencies of Silly Putty." Reseated and hopefully properly realigned, he began, speaking somewhat louder than before. "Mr. Hamilton, you are one of the architects of the park affair, are you not?"

"Yes, your honor."

"And how did you become involved, exactly?"

"Madison Weber was in need of help." Apprehension was playing foosball in the pit of my stomach. I fought to stay calm.

Chute's eyebrows gave away his growing curiosity. "So, you two cooked up a scheme."

Weber appeared set to speak out but I cut her off. "Not so, your honor. The girl had no prior knowledge the motorcycle club was backing her."

"But you knew, did you not, Mr. Hamilton, that the Scouts would be at the park?"

Shit! The judge was asking all the right questions. "Yes, I knew." I dared not glance at Zeb or Shifter, to witness their surprise and sense of betrayal.

"Why did Miss Weber call upon and choose you, Mr. Hamilton?"

"I can answer that," Madison shouted with urgency.

Chute shot her a look. "I'm asking Mr. Hamilton, Miss Weber. Rest assured, you'll have your chance."

With a shrug, I answered the judge's question honestly. "Don't rightly know. Probably desperate."

"Hardly," Madison blurted out. "The proof's in the pudding, your honor. The oak trees are still standing."

Exasperated, Chute thundered, *"But you're not, Miss Weber,* which is why we're all here *partaking this exercise!* You are familiar, are you not, Miss Weber, of proper decorum and procedure, of the phrase contempt-of-court and the ramifications thereof?"

Madison sat bewildered.

"In short...no more outbursts, young lady."

"Yes, sir."

"Thank you, Miss Weber. Now, Mr. Hamilton, I'm confused. Were all the club members...let me see..." Chute again ransacked his notes, "what was the name again...?"

"The Dry Dog Blues, sir."

Chute grunted, "Yes. Thank you, Mr. Hamilton. Now, were members aware of the Scout troop's involvement?"

I glanced at Zeb. A reflex action. One look was all it took. I was a dead-man walking. "No, your honor," responding nervously, "none of them knew."

Chute persisted, "If your motorcycle gang, forgive me, cycle club had known...that the young women were to be stampeded into the park to aid its defense and, I might add, be placed in harm's way...would they have agreed to such a course of action, Mr. Hamilton?"

"Excuse me, but that is speculative and argumentative, your honor." Juliet Spinnetti, standing in the far corner, had made her presence known.

Chute squinted. "And you are?"

Jule answered.

"And what capacity brings you to this inquiry, Ms. Spinnetti?"

"I'm third year at Drake Law and a friend of Mr. Hamilton, your honor."

Chute had a sly smile, his interest piqued again. "Graduation is near, I presume."

"Yes, sir. Two weeks." Jule was holding steady.

"Congratulations, young lady. Are you attending this hearing at Mr. Hamilton's request?"

"No, your honor. I'm here on my own...to show support."

"If I might be so bold, Ms. Spinnetti. Am I pronouncing that correctly?"

"Yes, your honor."

"What exactly is your relationship with Mr. Hamilton?"

From opposite sides of the room, Jule and I regarded one another. I was thinking—good question, judge.

"Ahhhh...girlfriend/boyfriend?" Jule replied with a pained look.

"Is that a statement or a question, Ms. Spinnetti?"

Unnerved, Juliet hesitantly offered, "I...I'm not sure."

The meeting hall exploded with a good-natured laugh.

The judge waited for the crowd to settle down. "Well now, you've heard from your legal support, Mr. Hamilton. Care to answer the question? Would the Dry Dog Blues have gone along?"

"Don't know."

"Take a guess."

"Probably not."

"Thank you, Mr. Hamilton. Ms. Spinnetti is quite right. Your answer is speculative, but it helps boil down the soup, so to speak, that you and you alone planned the confrontation on the eleventh."

Wow. Chute had me pinpointed. I heard the distinct echoing sound—*clank!*—of a prison cell door closing behind me. I shivered and spoke out. "The truth, sir. Last Friday morning I had little idea what was about to befall us all."

"But you envisioned the possibility of what actually occurred, did you not?" Chute's eyebrows were doing jumping jacks.

I was grasping for a defense. "Yes, but that was one of many scenarios, one of many *maybes*."

"The motorcycle club meeting was held when?" Chute was flipping through paperwork.

I elected to help him out; anything to aid my cause.

"Wednesday, the ninth, Your Honor."

"Yes, the ninth. Miss Weber had asked for assistance, and that evening the club agreed in principal and directed you to work out the particulars. Is that not true, Mr. Hamilton?"

"Not quite so clear-cut, your honor. Madison didn't ask for backing, per se. She said Troop 822 was going to try and save the park. I realized this was important to her, that she was making an overture, to make me aware, that I might pick up a bat and get into the game. But there was never a *please help*."

"Two days, young man. You had forty eight hours to consider your, as you say, many maybes. Yet you confided in no one."

The judge was like a boa constrictor wrapping around, upping the pressure. "I gave serious thought to laying it all out to Zeb Story."

"Why?"

"He's our leader in the Blues. I trust his instinct."

"Were you aware that his daughter, Ana, was a Scout and directly involved?"

"No. Only Weber. I didn't know who the other girls were."

"Seems like a strange omission on your part, Mr. Alexander Hamilton."

"Big time, your honor." If I conveyed a haunted look, it was right on target. "I have no excuse."

Chute again grunted. "Thus you elected, I take it, not to confide in Mr. Story."

"Yes."

"So, prior to Friday, you had confided in no one."

I peered over at Jule. With a subtle hand motion, she was signaling—no, don't.

To answer honestly loomed as incriminating as hell. But why not? My goose was cooked anyway. Chute was right. I owed them all the truth. I said, "One exception."

"Meaning?"

"I contacted Miss Spinnetti, your honor. On the phone."

The judge redirected. "Care to divulge your conversation with Mr. Hamilton, Ms. Spinnetti?"

I assumed she was considering a legal stonewall, a quasi-lawyer-client confidentiality, so I called out, "Tell him, Jule. If you don't, I will."

She sighed. "He wanted to know Iowa law pertaining to kidnapping."

An ominous undercurrent rumbled throughout the room. Any sympathy I might have garnered earlier was gone. Chute nodded and said, "Thank you, Ms. Spinnetti." Returning my direction, he asked the obvious, "Why the stampede, Mr. Hamilton? Why involve the Scouts at all? Why not simply ride your motorcycles into the grove and make a stand?"

I didn't have to answer that one. Harlin Shifter cleared his throat and mumbled a faint but clearly heard, "Timber."

HARLIN

Smirking broke out in the crowded room. It did not go unnoticed as Chute, clearly annoyed, directed his attention to the source. "Your name, sir!"

"Harlin Shifter."

With his shattered ribs wrapped and mending, he appeared cockeyed and shriveled. Bent at the waist, using a cane for support, anticipating a twinge of pain with every move, Shifter's best mood was surly.

His name rang a warning bell. Scrutinizing an obvious adversary, Chute noted, "According to the reports, Mr. Shifter, you apparently ran over a Mr. Milo Spur with your motorcycle causing bodily..."

"Ran over hell, the moron leaped smack dab in front of me."

"You are aware the seriousness of your position, Mr. Shifter...of a pending charge of aggravated assault?"

Shifter returned a withering glare. "You gonna charge me, Judge? Get in line. Right now it aggravates me to try to pick up a toothbrush. Every move I make aggravates, and God knows who's paying for all this medical shit." Harlin kept on, babbling to himself mostly. "The shovel's trashed. Bent frame. The tanks, the new paint job...dented all to hell. If Spur's lookin' for payback and wants me rounded up and locked up, well, go on and unleash the bloodhounds; he's the least of my problems."

"This hearing sympathizes with your physical condition, Mr. Shifter. It also recognizes no cause for coarse language. You will refrain, sir."

Milo Spur, seated across the room, shouted, "Damn, Shifter, I'm at the tree. Chains dug in. Wood chips are flying. I get a sensation sumpin's not right. I turn, and Lord-o-mighty, here you come charging at me on that chopper bike from hell. I jumped from shear fright. If I'd had time to extract the saw, I'd of pared your ass."

Chute allowed the exchange to carry on, hoping to let some emotion play out.

Harlin nearly spit. "And if I'd wanted to run you down, you'd be sportin' Dunlap tread-marks 'long the bridge of your nose."

Robin Emerson had heard enough. Without thinking as to the time or place, she lashed out, "It's always you against the world, isn't it Harlin. You screwed up. You're the perp here, you...you self-centered jerk. Take some damned responsibility!" She abruptly shut up, embarrassed, once again sensing the spotlight and the stares. Stress had been building for days: the frightening storm, the kids being severely hurt, the bike club, the in-fighting with Wayne. She was a pressure-release valve past the max—exploding.

Using his cane, Shifter stood, wincing from the effort. Standing or sitting, he could never find a comfort zone. Ignoring Chief Rolli Guy's reproaching everyone to settle down, Shifter, shaking his fist, let fly at me and Zeb. "Told you two, didn't I. Warned ya not to let her in. Any of you blockheads listen? No! Less than a week she's in the club, Story. Less than seven, Hamilton. Half the guys tore up in the hospital, half headin' for the slammer."

Listening to Shifter lash out, Robin didn't know to laugh or cry. She was so conflicted. This—this—guy. Harlin Shifter was an original, an enigma. Robin peered over at him smoldering like a worn out fire. One fact was worth remembering. Last Friday, he had been there for them all. The man had put *everything* on the line. Badly injured, he'd refused to leave the park. He may be an pompous, bullheaded, pain in the keister, but he'd been there when courage mattered most.

Judge Cyrus Chute gaveled the assembled back to order. Lightheartedly, he said, "Ms. Emerson. Mr. Shifter. Are you two aware you're on the same team?"

As laughter subsided he marked the two adversaries: plenty of gender animosity, but not without a wee bit of dancing in the dark. Chute chided himself to focus. His inquiry was fluttering off in so many digressions, Shakespeare might be needed to pen a resolution. He fixed a heavy stare at Harlin Shifter, silently burrowing into an angry psyche. Thirty years on the bench, he had seen them all: pathological liars, the clueless and uncaring, the incorrigibles—the list went on. But no, the injured biker bore little relationship with that criminal tribe. Chute tossed him a line. "You're burning bridges, Mr. Shifter."

The biker, acknowledging the judge with a grumble, took the bait. "None of us in the Blues had intentions of harming anyone." He pointed at me. "Our Revolutionary War ringleader over there shouts out marching orders. Story and I head out to stop Shimmer's crew from downing the oak. Terrain's hidden and rough. In my rearview I see Zeb go down. I meant to blow by Milo. Spook him. He jumped. I lost control trying to avoid him. I never meant to clip him. The last second, I tried to bail and jack-knifed my ass into the hospital."

Chute thought, *Not an apology to warm the cockles of the heart,* but it was a start. He pointed at Shifter and Milo Spur. "You two can let the courts settle liability. You can sit on opposite aisles and assign judge or jury to arbitrate grievances. But there's another road you both might consider. Holster your pride, reconcile a peg, and see where that winds up. Just a reminder, boys, a peace pipe is a whole lot cheaper than an attorney." Chute let the admonishment sink in. One could hope. Okay, one down and one to go. "Now, Mr. Shifter."

"Now what, Judge?"

Chute cocked his head at Robin. She was standing resolute, defiant.

Annoyed, Shifter recognized what the judge was after; encouraging a truce with this gal. Staring out at Robin Emerson, he took stock of himself. Perhaps the real annoyance here was his boneheaded, continued self-denial over the attraction (right or wrong) he felt for this woman. She was an itch, and he had never been one to let feelings fester. Judge Chute and Robin Emerson had him completely off-guard. In the fervor of the moment, anger gave way to wistful longing.

Self-absorbed and heedless of the consequences, Harlin Shifter spoke slowly and clearly.

"When lilacs last in the dooryard bloom'd,

Amidst the spring-fed plains, we'll find higher ground."

Not many, including Robin, at first understood exactly what was said. A few jaws dropped.

Chute smiled. "Walt Whitman. Nicely fashioned, Mr. Shifter."

With that, the judge recast. "So, Mr. Hamilton, I take it then the Scouts were an insurance policy?"

Still mesmerized by the Chute/Shifter exchange, it took a moment to realize the judge was back in my corner. "The club's had a few run-ins with Shimmer's boys. Nothing serious, but with just us Blues in the park, well...we'd probably be a good target. They'd have surely called our bluff. We needed to win the day, your honor. Being with the Scouts was the best-case scenario."

"One final question, Mr. Hamilton. You're not employed at Heartland Ironworks. By your own admission, you don't know the Scouts. Why go to all this trouble?"

Folks leaned *en masse* my direction awaiting my reply. Chute's question: the big one. I weighed my words carefully. "I envisioned a future. The trees rooted up. The road built. A future of looking in the mirror and growing tired of asking myself why, when I was given a chance to right a wrong, I elected to do nothing; another notch on my belt of ever-lowering expectations. I didn't want that to happen, your honor. In truth, sir, I'm horrified over what occurred at

Wildnut Park. But deep down, I feel betrayed that a monster storm blew-up and destroyed my best intentions."

Chute's squint was taking the measure of me. A new respect? I doubted that. My time was at an end. He was curt and to-the-point. "I'm not sure the law's going to factor your vision and betrayal into consideration, Mr. Hamilton. Furthermore, sir, those badly hurt were not victimized purely by coincidence and bad luck. What say you?"

"No, your honor. I certainly played a heavy hand."

"Quite right, Mr. Hamilton. I appreciate your testimony today, son. Now then...speaking of the afflicted." Chute had taken note of two new attendees, one of whom he had expected. "At this time I'd like to ask Dr. Solomon Jolly to bring us up-to-date on those injured and hospitalized." The judge acknowledged the late arrivals standing close to the door. "If you please, Dr. Jolly."

They had quietly slipped into the meeting hall as Chute was attempting to make sense of me and Shifter. Joining Dr. Jolly stood a tall, slender blonde. Everyone recognized Summer Hook.

DOC

"Thank you, Judge Chute. Good afternoon, everyone. County hospital admitted ten individuals following the storm last Friday, May 11..."

He wore light gray dress slacks with a short-sleeve, white cotton shirt. No tie. He was tall, slight in frame, pale-complexioned, and hardly aging in his early sixties. Curing ills and mending bones for many a year, our own Dr. J was as much a fixture in Sugar City as was the sale barn, the pharmacy that anchored the town square, or the old brick high school. Rumors had run rampant the past few days. The crowded hall was all ears as he took the lead.

"...three of whom remain hospitalized." Jolly gazed around the room. "Before moving on, I'd like to commend our Emergency Medical Team, all of whom, I see, are here today. Also William Ribbs, who was in the grove when the tree fell and, as a former combat medic, provided immediate, essential aid. There were no fatalities that morning, but without the professionalism of these folks, there very well might have been."

A smattering of applause caught fire and grew.

Judge Chute had done his Sugar City History homework. Searching out Bobbi Brinkerhoff, he noted, "Heroics yet again, young lady."

Bobbi took a few seconds to comprehend Chute's reference but she'd been through this before: her last-second shot off the backboard. "That was years ago, sir."

"Never underestimate the lasting joy and pride that can emanate from a ball in flight, Ms. Brinkerhoff. It's good to see you here and make your acquaintance."

Jolly was set to continue when Ribbs spoke up. "Pardon, Doc...Judge, if I may steal a minute?"

"Dr. Jolly?"

"By all means."

"Go right on ahead, son," Chute said. "Take your time."

I was all ears. This was unprecedented. Will never spoke up in a crowd.

"I've been harboring guilt over last Friday. The motorcycle club had planned to ride earlier that morning. I was late to the rendezvous point, which made us all late. Had we confronted Lonnie and his crew before the Scouts showed up, well...maybe a deal might have been reached, avoiding all that happened."

Chute halted him there. "Fine, Mr. Ribbs, but police reports and testimony today abound with *if*'s and *only*'s. We're not here to..."

"I understand, Judge. What I want to explain, especially with all these folks here today, is the reason I was late. Last Friday was a planned pet show-and-tell at the nursing home where I work. Believing the confrontation at Wildnut would end quickly without incident, I had my ferret with me. I'd had trouble at home that morning finding where he was sleeping... that's why I was late. In the storm tragedy that followed, I forgot about him. I returned much later to find my motorcycle crushed under a pile of heavy limbs and his carrying cage in pieces. There was no sign of him. It's been three days, your honor. If he was killed on impact there's a good chance he was carried off by a predator, but maybe he survived and wandered off. Wouldn't be the first time. He's harmless. So, if anyone sees him, put water out and call me. Thanks, your honor. Sorry to use up time for this."

"This ferret have a name, Mr. Ribbs?"

"Yes, sir. Slacker Red."

"Well then," Chute surmised, leaning back and clasping his hands at the back of his head, "in light of your admission, Mr. Ribbs, I suppose it is supportable to blame this entire confounding affair on the late-rising weasel."

Ribbs stood silent.

Effie Poole calmly inquired, "For the record, your honor?"

Caught off-guard, Chute tended to his recorder. "By all means, Ms. Poole. *For* the record."

Light laughter sprinkled throughout the room.

"Been a tough go this week, eh, Mr. Ribbs?"

"A bit bent out of shape from Mother Nature's pliers, your honor."

"Well put. Hope you find your pet, young man."

"Me too. Thank you, sir."

"Now, Dr. Jolly, if you'd be so kind."

"Yes, of course. Seven of those admitted last Friday have been released and are here today. Rachel Bradbury and Ana Story were tended to for minor cuts and abrasions. Both are in good health. X-rays showed Madison Weber to have a broken ankle. That was set. She was treated for shock, dehydration, and multiple lacerations to the face and neck." The good doctor bore a casual demeanor, but possessed expressive, darting eyes that lit up discourse. He disregarded his hand-held notes to locate the girl. "By her own account she appears ghoulish. But little stitching was required, her facial cuts are not deep, the trauma being epidermal, akin to road rash. Other than a lower lip indenture, scarring will be faint to nonexistent. She shows no signs of infection. With time, and I hope you don't mind me saying this, young lady, she'll bounce back as pretty as ever."

Pretty caught Madison by surprise. She never thought herself pretty. No one had spoken such words. Well, maybe mom and dad, but they don't count. "Bit of a stretch, Doctor J."

Jolly knowingly smiled.

Standing close by, Riley Blue whispered, "Hardly."

Madison shot him a glare. Riley drew back. That boy!

Jolly was moving on. "Jessi Bradbury suffered from emotional stress, as did most involved, abetted by cuts, abrasions, and a fracture of the right clavicle. She'll be in a sling for six weeks, then it's back to the violin, Jessi." Jolly grinned.

Jessi spoke up, "I don't play the violin."

"Well, you'll be able to start. That's what's important." The good doctor's smile faded. "Zeb Story, Harlin Shifter, and Milo Spur have also been released. Mr. Story was admitted unconscious; his life spared by the actions of those tending him. The EMTs administered CPR and prevented internal drowning. He was treated for a severe head wound requiring stitching, but a CT scan showed no skull fractures nor any intracranial bleeding. He still suffers from a second-degree concussion and amnesia. His vital signs are good. With time the bruise to his brain will heal." Locating Zeb, Dr. Jolly noted the obvious, "You're a lucky man, Mr. Story. You have a lot to be thankful for."

Zeb stood stoic, acknowledging the doctor's remarks, but remained silent.

"Milo Spur broke his leg. His fractured tibia is casted and on the mend. Keep the weight off, Milo. Harlin Shifter was treated for three broken ribs and a severe laceration to his left leg. Currently he is an outpatient, attended to for infection and pain." Jolly found Shifter. "It'll be a slow process, Harlin. 'Take it easy' will be your mantra for a while. The ribs are set and braced. You'll come through ship-shape. Like Mr. Story, I'd take a moment now and then to thank your lucky star."

Jolly asked for a glass of water. We all knew it wasn't going to get better and our general practitioner was never one to shy away. "Lily Starr nearly died. She arrived in pain and shock with a punctured, collapsed lung. Procedures to remedy her condition have been successful. She is breathing normally, but remains hospitalized. Pulmonary contusions have caused infection, and she is being monitored for signs of pneumonia." Solomon stole a napkin from the table in front and wiped his brow. "Don't mean to scare you folks. Her condition is listed as fair. I have been with Lily. She's talking and alert, but has very little stamina. There is cause for concern, but her doctors and I expect recovery. In layman's terms, we're covering all the bases and leaving nothing to chance."

I gazed over at Madison. She appeared to almost wilt from the suspense. Our sense of relief over Lily was short-lived.

"Both Gordon Estey and Autumn Hook were life-flighted last Friday to University Hospital in Iowa City. Gordon is undergoing surgery to repair three vertebral fractures. I don't have to explain to any of you folks that this is serious business.

Dislocated vertebrae can damage the spinal cord, leading to permanent paralysis."

Someone shouted, "What are his chances, Doc?"

"I'm an optimistic son-of-a-gun. Gordon's strong as an ox. Sixty percent says he'll walk again. Right now, though, it's too early for a long term prognosis. Fractures pushing on nerves cause numbness. Swelling needs to come down. Bone fragments may be a problem up ahead. Scar tissue will be an issue. No sense getting technical. In a few weeks' time, we'll know more. Listen, folks, I'm well aware that it took a chain saw and six able-bodied men to manually lift that oak limb to free Gordon. How this man was able to physically raise himself to free the girls is a mystery; medically speaking, it is an impossibility. A miracle took place in Wildnut Park. Now we're working diligently for another."

While the doctor took a moment to collect himself, Chute asked, "Care for a chair, Dr. Jolly?"

"No, thank you. We prefer standing. Now then, I believe this gal next to me needs no introduction. Do you want to say a few words now, Summer, or wait?"

"Now, I think."

"Okay. The floor is yours."

"Hi, everyone. I'm here for my sister, Autumn. She wrote down some stuff she asked me to read to you."

Jolly was right. Nearly all recognized Sugar City's favorite first daughter, but no one recalled Summer as she stood before them now, Amish-like in a long, plain, dark blue dress, her hair tied tightly back up in a bun. The image folks carried from the past was the carefree, captivating, willowy blonde commanding the basketball court. Now, looking run-down with head bowed and shoulders slumped, she began relaying her sister's message:

> First off, I'm so grateful to Mr. Estey for saving my life; also Lily and Rachel for being wonder women when dragging me free, and Mr. Ribbs for patching me up. Sorry about all the screaming. Next, I'm overwhelmed by all the balloons, cards, and flowers. Thank you all. My room at the hospital looks like Connie's Floral right before Valentine's Day.

Her composure dissolving in tears, Summer spoke barely above a whisper: *Lastly...Go Troop.*

"That's it, Dr. Jolly." Summer seemed to flinch as if struck by a phantom blow.

Solomon extended a sympathetic hand, held on, and addressed the hearing. "Yesterday evening, Autumn's doctors and her folks Dorothy and Earl, concurred to wait no longer. Autumn's leg wound had deteriorated and become life-threatening. A BKA, a below-the-knee amputation, was performed. The surgery was successful. Autumn is listed in serious but stable condition."

The commons room reacted with stunned silence. Only a few oh-no's were heard. I watched Madison stagger on over to Ana and Rachel, the three barely able to hold one another upright. I felt Chute's stare and didn't dare face him. I wanted to run and escape this stifling room. An ocean of guilt and anger swept over me. I wanted to run until my lungs burst.

Jolly continued on with the lack of circulation, dead tissue, infection, gangrene, peg-legs, and prosthetics. Attempting a positive slant, he detailed Autumn's surgeon's determination to mend arterial and ligament trauma and save the knee joint and the importance of that. I barely heard a word. Chute could have screamed, "You'll get twenty years for this, Alexander Hamilton!" I'd have responded, Make it solitary. But he didn't and the hearing rolled on.

MADDY

Cyrus Chute pondered Madison Weber. She was perched on a tall-backed footstool near the far wall, holding hands with another Scout. The youngster had been rocked hard by Jolly's disclosures. He wanted her story, but saw the need to tread lightly. "Miss Weber," he spoke kindly, "as with Mr. Hamilton, I'd like to understand why you chose to take part last Friday? Why you actually led the way?"

Madison was in another world. Her focus was gone. The heartbreak over Gordon and Autumn was too much. Her worst fears. Her responsibility. Her fault. She craved a trapdoor beneath her feet, an escape hatch to crawl down and vanish forever.

With the girl lost in tears of despair, Chute lifted his voice a notch and repeated his question.

A shadow shuffled close, gently shook her shoulder, and held on. Madison arched her neck to peer into the face of her comforter. Riley Blue. They were forehead to forehead.

He whispered, "It'll be okay. Hang in there." He let go, swiftly backtracking.

Riley?! She looked like a reject from Frankenstein's lab, yet here he was again in her corner. She was regarding him in wonder as Chute tried a third time. "Miss Weber?"

Madison yielded to the judge's persistence. "The old trees and my dad. To help them both."

Judge Chute then made a move that Effie Poole later said she'd never witnessed in all her years as his legal aide and courtroom recorder. With a grunt, he stood, ambled around the front table, made his way to the rear of the room, and presented Madison his handkerchief, which was both needed and gratefully accepted. Without a word, he about-faced and lumbered back to the dais. It was a gesture long-remembered after the hearing.

"From the reports I've read, you're not the only one accepting blame, Miss Weber. It might interest you to know Police Chief Guy has confided his own remorse at failing to clear the park prior to the storm. Mr. Shimmer regrets even showing up that morning with his crew and equipment, given the pessimistic weather forecast. We've just heard from Mr. Ribbs, and there is no telling Mr. Hamilton's second thoughts over his role." Chute hesitated, searching for the words. "Accepting responsibility for one's actions is a sign of stalwartness, Miss Weber."

Madison, listening closely, simply nodded.

The judge proceeded, warming to the task. "A great American once wrote: 'Broken eggs can never be mended, and

the longer the breaking proceeds, the more will be broken.'"
With a knowing smile, he inquired, "Care to venture as to the
source, Miss Weber?"

For whatever reason, Madison flashed back to her dad on
Saturday mornings, wearing his goofy apron in the kitchen,
following along with the TV and making a mess. She took a
stab. "Julia Child?"

Cyrus threw his head back and rocked with laughter. He
couldn't help it. "Close! I speak of Abraham Lincoln, young
lady." The judge struggled to return to proper decorum,
saying, "I cite the quote as a reminder, Ms. Weber. Though
Lincoln spoke on the preservation of the Union, your quest
to save the oaks proceeded on that same certainty. Do you
follow?"

She wasn't sure, but answered, "Yes, sir."

"Very well then." The Scout appeared to him to be
regaining composure. He, on the other hand, was losing his.
He was still chuckling over Julia and Abe. When you thought
about it, there *was* a facial resemblance. This uncanny and
disarming child. "Now, Miss Weber, your father you say.
Elaborate, please."

"Your Honor." Paul Weber intervened, "If I may..."

"Dad! Let me finish. I can do this."

Paul nodded to his daughter and allowed the inevitable.

Madison felt a kinetic spark and silently scolded herself,
Be a *Scout*, runt. She followed up, "My dad's the financial whiz

246 | ROBERT ESPENSCHEID JR.

at Heartland. He was in a funk over his job, the trees being destroyed, the bridge not being built. I wanted to help."

"Bridge you say."

"Yeah. A better way for the new road to go that got ousted."

"And what was your father's reaction to the planned protest?"

"I...I never told him my ideas."

"Why?" As soon as he said it, Cyrus knew it was a dumb question.

"Duh. He'd have deep-sixed the protest big time. No need to be involved, Madison. I will handle this my own way. A company matter. Not your concern. Typical dad stuff."

"So you asked the Scout troop to assist?"

"Yeah. We had a meeting on summer projects to make money and help the town. I figured saving Wildnut Park fit right in...and those trees are like a legacy. Nobody mows down a gift like that. I even backed up my plan with the Girl Scout Law."

Chute was piqued. "Meaning?"

Madison almost smiled, thinking how proud Lily would be of her as she said, "Part of the law says: Use resources wisely. Make the world a better place."

"Aha. So you are opting for a Girl Scout defense, Ms. Weber."

"I can think of none better, your honor."

Chute leaned back in his chair. His admiration for this young woman was growing with each exchange. "I have a grand-niece your age, Miss Weber, also a Scout. I'm aware that your law also makes reference to respecting others, respecting authority. Does it not?"

"Yes, your honor." Madison answered, disheartened.

The two of them paused. Chute scanned his notes. He'd lost his train of thought.

Madison, taking advantage of the lapse, pitched in with the *word game;* an exercise she fondly shared with classmates in ninth-grade English. It was a silly gesture to be sure, popping out of her mouth without forethought; an inner longing, perhaps, to distance the terror of last Friday and return to normalcy, if just for a moment. She meant no arrogance or spite. "I stand admonished, your honor. Admonish. That's my *key* word this week. Our lit teacher assigns a new word each Monday. We're supposed to find... ahhh...add it to our vocab. Everyday speaking stuff. Mrs. Rose says we need to wean ourselves away from *shut ups, likes, and whatevers.*"

A nervous playfulness swept the room.

"Harrumph. Glad I was so accommodating, Miss Weber. Your teacher is to be commended."

"I'll relay that, sir."

Chute, still looking down at his paperwork, airing complete nonchalance, replied, "Well...whatever."

The commons room exploded with laughter.

I held Madison in awe. She had whipped up a catharsis. I thought, *We can't alter reality. Hurt and sorrow had a stranglehold on this proceeding. Nevertheless, we can't forsake the small pluses, the smiles, the reason we're all on this green planet: to make the best of it.*

She and the judge had brewed up a reaffirmation, and for a twinkling of an eye, the joy of the day-to-day.

Having found what he was searching for, the judge was back on track. "One last question, Ms. Weber. What was your Scout leader's...a Ms. Jessi Bradbury, I believe...reaction to the planned protest?"

"She trashed it. Total taboo, your honor. We...I mean, I went ahead alone."

"Thank you, young lady. I appreciate your testimony here today as well as your forthrightness. Try on that word next week, Miss Weber."

The crowd elicited a light-hearted murmur. More importantly, the judge scored a half-grin from Madison. She was peering over at her parents. Her mom was wearing her worried look. Her dad offered a thumbs-up. She had done her best.

THE OAKS

Zeb Story was harboring Judge Chute and his so-called inquest with growing impatience. Enough of this beating up on thirteen-year-olds. Where were the suits? Guilt was flying around the room like an angry nest of hornets. Hamilton looked dead and gone. Why the hell wasn't someone pointing an electric cattle-prod at the real culprit behind this train wreck: Heartland Ironworks?' Stewing, he eyed a seemingly contented Dick Lester with malice.

The wait was over.

"Mr. Lester." The judge's voice rang out like the bell to the main event. "Tell me, sir, how many acorns does a white oak tree produce?"

The oddball query caught folks off-guard, including Heartland's plant supervisor, who had been sitting expectantly and now forced a half-smile, not quite comprehending. "I'm not sure I follow."

"Oh come now, Mr. Lester. It's a plain and simple question. For one growing season, how many acorns? On one tree."

His composure tweaked, Lester dumped the smile. "I don't fathom why..."

"Ten thousand, Mr. Lester," Chute interrupted, "give or take a few."

Lester sat perplexed. Chute asked, "From a seedling, how many years must an oak thrive before flowering and producing an acorn, Mr. Lester?"

"Sir, this line of questioning has no bearing..."

"Twenty-five, Mr. Lester, give or take a few. Now then, could you inform the assembled as to the acorn's importance, sir? What's its purpose?"

The head of Heartland eyed Chute with cold, blue hatred—*How dare this country bumpkin publicly embarrass him*—angrily declaring, "I'm no longer taking part in these proceedings."

"Food, protein, Mr. Lester!" Chute shouted, throwing himself forward into a half-stance, bracing himself straight-armed, knuckles on the table. "Oaks feed the forest. White-

and black-tailed deer, hogs, raccoons, squirrels, rodents, quail, pheasant, woodpeckers, jays, wild turkeys all partake the feast. An annual acorn crop determines how many animals survive the winter, Mr. Lester." The judge glowed crimson; his heart pounding.

Dick Lester turned to his associate sitting beside him with stacks of bulging legal folders, who simply shrugged his shoulders.

"I find it disturbing, Mr. Lester, your failure at answering my inquiries."

"I do not wish to give credence to your charade," Lester spat with contempt.

"A strong man confined to a wheelchair. A young woman losing a leg. Another fighting for the breath of life. This is hardly a charade, sir."

Judge Cyrus Chute sat back down, his arms entwined tightly across his chest. There was a sadness in his voice. "A man who sets forth to destroy had best know his adversary: his strongholds, his history...lest he be smote in return."

Lester sat silent.

Cyrus sighed. There were others attending to confirm, perhaps even add to the drama, but he recognized folks now had a pretty good idea what had transpired last Friday—and why. Business concerns and property legalities awaited a future venue. "Before we adjourn, I'd like to ask Mr. Richard Lester and his associate to remain a spell."

23
REVELATION

Cyrus rose. "All of you who have attended today, particularly those giving voice to these proceedings, I'd like to thank..."

"Judge Chute! Wait! If I may, sir, I wish to add a statement before everyone disperses."

He eyed me impatiently. "Now's not the time for some sort of blanket apology, Mr. Hamilton."

"No, no, it's not that. This is of a different nature, your honor. I won't take long. Less than a minute."

Still standing, he sighed. "Say your piece, Mr. Hamilton."

"Thank you. I'd like to make sure what I say becomes part of the official Record."

The judge beckoned to his recorder. "By all means, let this be on record, Mrs. Poole." She nodded, then smiled encouragement my direction.

I stood. I'd thought about this opportunity and what I'd do. There was no turning back now, and if I was determined to soar off the high dive, I might as well make it a somersaulting spectacular. A hard rock bottom awaited, regardless. "That morning as the storm hit and the tree was crashing down, I...I...froze. My body was encased like that of a cemented flagpole. As the oak was falling directly on top of me, I heard a shrieking. Shrill screams unlike any other..."

"You heard the wind, young man." Chute was already impatient. "It's been estimated that the wind shear from the storm's downburst exceeded 120 mph. I doubt, Mr. Hamilton, you've been subjected to such a tempest."

"No, I have not, sir, and you are correct that the wind's fury had a voice of its own. If I might add, not one I care to relive. But this...this explosion of sound rose above the gale's roar, sir. A heavenly sound. A cry that grew as the tree fell."

The packed commons room was silent. Waiting.

"Perhaps it was those around you. The Scouts wailing and running for their lives, perhaps the town's warning siren, Mr. Hamilton."

I took a deep breath, trying to remain calm. I *had* to see this through. What I was trying to put into words was a consciousness that haunted me that terrible morning and haunts me still. "As the tree was tumbling from the sky, everything unfolding slowed as if my mind was attempting to forestall the catastrophe. I heard the terrified Scouts, the ripping and shredding of tree branches, perhaps the faint tornado siren, too. But atop all the chaos there was this shrieking...a cosmic aria...I heard it clearly."

Reluctantly expectant, Chute asked, "And you're venturing what, Mr. Hamilton?"

My mouth was dry. I barely managed to swallow. "It was the rooted trees surrounding us, your honor. I believe I heard the trees screaming."

The judge's eyebrows shot straight up. "Trees screaming, you say."

"Yes, sir. The oaks screaming. And...," glancing at the recorder, "I'd like that fact written into the record."

Mrs. Poole acknowledged me with a discreet wink.

I surveyed the room. I had expected a chorus of disbelief and laughter. There was a smattering of whispers, but for the most part, folks remained mute. Chute provided me an odd look but elected to defer any added commentary. At the time, I thought it strange.

"So noted, son. Now, I appreciate all of you taking time today. As for those who provided testimony," his eyes locating familiar faces, "it's been an education. As I noted prior to Mr. Hamilton's last-minute disclosure, I wish to have a final word in private with the Heartland representatives. Mr. Lester, if you please and Mr. Hamilton, I'd refrain from planning any distant excursions if I were you."

"This is my home, your honor."

"Good answer, son. Well then, good day to you all and..."

"One more intrusion if I may, your honor." Dammit. More needed to be said. With everyone together here at the center; this was my one and only chance—and I had little left to lose, anyway.

"Come now, Alexander, these folk have lives to..."

"*Judge Chute!* One final minute. Please."

Those shuffling about readying to leave noted the edge in my voice and stood still. My brash plea had Chute off-balance. He hesitated. I took advantage and called out, "Most of us there in the grove last Friday wound up hospitalized. None of us, I'm pretty sure, have been able to venture back to the park. These past few days, there have been rumors floating about. Unexpected revelations, your honor. Are you aware, sir? Care to speculate?"

The judge studied me. Suddenly I knew. He was more than aware. He'd seen! I rushed, "Sir, you lectured earlier about truth and the importance of closure. Surely, even rumors rate an airing here today, a consideration."

"Mr. Hamilton, how might you..."

I smiled. "It's a small town, your honor."

Cyrus Chute was at a crossroad. He'd decided early on not to raise the mystery. He wasn't convinced this hearing was the proper forum. Now, what with screaming trees and questioning stares, avoidance was no longer possible. He sensed he was teetering on a narrow ledge above ground with a fair chance of toppling over and looking the fool. On the bench his professional principles were grounded in staying with the facts. But the truth, Miss Madison Weber's greased pig, the truth was that this entire episode fascinated him, and if there were unexplained forces afoot, well—perhaps it was fitting, even essential, to let them have a run. Allow these Sugar City town folk to draw their own conclusions. "All right,

Alexander Hamilton, I'll bow to your stubborn inquiry. If anyone wishes to leave, feel free."

No one moved.

"Okay then." Chute felt himself captaining through uncharted waters, but surprisingly content that this final act was commanding center stage.

"For the record, your honor?"

Effie's question added a forgotten weight, but only for a moment. "Yes, Mrs. Poole, for the record. Let the chickens roost."

Everyone grabbed a seat.

The Judge began. "We heard earlier from Dr. Jolly, and as serious as the injured are, the plausibility exists that a number of those within the tree grove Friday morning faced certain death. I'm referring to Lily Starr, Rachel Bradbury, Autumn Hook, Gordon Estey, and yes, you too Mr. Hamilton." Chute paused, adding to the dramatic effect. He hesitated, for he felt an old-time sermon taking shape, an allure he was wont to draw upon. He silently chided himself to desist. There was no need to rise to the pulpit. Not yet. "Yes, they'd have lost their lives had not...how best to put this...had not Providence intervened."

Sitting or standing, Chute's audience was a giant question mark.

"On the evening of the eleventh, following the storm, the attorney general called and asked me to intercede as his intermediary. The following day, Saturday, Sheriff Guy, myself, and two county conservation officers gathered at Wildnut Park."

Chute took a moment for a sip of water. Folks acted like sunflowers, tilting toward him, craning their necks to catch every word.

"I'm simply relating what I saw. The tree, the old sentinel oak, that was uprooted in the storm and sent spiraling into the grove...never hit the ground. Not completely."

An edgy silence reigned throughout the commons.

The Judge explained. "Falling from the sky, the big oak got tangled to a halt by the trees still standing. The main trunk was precariously wedged some twenty feet from the ground. During the confusion and urgency after the storm, what with the massive entanglement of branches, the darkness, no one took notice. This past Saturday, we all took care venturing around a dangerous situation. From ground view, even with much of the greenery blown gone, it was next-to-impossible to ascertain how and where the oak was caught. Later that same evening, at home, I was notified by county conservation that the Great White had finally broken free and had plunged completely to the ground. Two of their fellows standing guard were lucky not to be added to the hospital rolls. Even from twenty feet, the ground shook on impact. The yellow stakes left by police officers Friday morning that designated where the injured were found and treated by emergency personnel, and I again refer to Ms. Starr, Hook, Bradbury, and Mr. Estey...well... those wooden markers were pulverized. The trunk measured eighteen foot around. No one would have survived such a crushing blow."

My knees buckled. I felt a cold chill. I needed to sit. Not seeking a response from anyone in particular, I blurted out, "How's that possible?"

"Not my place to judge fate, be it heaven-sent or otherwise," Chute responded. "But allow me to say this much."

Further attempts of his own to stem from sermonizing failed. So be it. He was a religious man with no qualms at representing and interpreting spiritual forces. His wife, God bless her, might chastise his pontificating at times, but not now, not here.

"I know an acre or two of Iowa's past as I'm sure you folks do. It's probable that grove of oaks were seedlings about the time this state joined the Union in the 1840s. Think about that. If trees could talk: a young hardwood forest with a bird's eye view, overlooking pristine prairie. But history can be turbulent. Those trees grew amid the settling of the land, the growth of family farms, factories and towns. Wood was needed for houses and business. Land was needed for growing feed. Winter sleet, lightning fires, tornados, and summer storms, the like of which you just experienced, took a toll. No one knows the complete history of that timber out there, but certainly, from time to time these past one hundred fifty years, stewards stepped forward, preventing the saw, the plow, and the torch from extinguishing forever, that band of oak. And now, here in 2001, at the edge of the new millennium, with suburban

258 | ROBERT ESPENSCHEID JR.

homes and industrial development on the rise, another steps forward; one fourteen-year-old Madison Weber. Another champion now added to the rolls of those defenders who rose up before her."

The judge stood and ended the hearing. "Thus, if Mr. Hamilton heard the old oaks screaming to find the strength to slow and cradle their uprooted sentinel, far be it for me to cast denial his direction. Maybe...just maybe...those trees, protected for decades, decided it was time to give something back. And that the lives of five precious young daughters was not a bad place to start."

Effie Poole asked, "For the record, your honor?"

Chute replied, "Word for word. Good day to you folks."

24
THE BLUES

Folks filed out slowly, both saddened and bewildered. We'd all gotten more than we bargained for. I hung back and waited. I needed to clear the air with Zeb over my entangling his daughter, Ana, at Wildnut Park. He'd be gunning for me.

We soon found ourselves remaining alone together right outside the commons. Our confrontation took a back seat as we listened, transfixed as Chute tore into Dick Lester behind closed door. We didn't make out every word, but we caught the drift. The judge spoke in a harsh, uncompromising manner that had hardly registered at the hearing.

"...arrogance, shortsightedness, and ignorance...set in motion a sequence of events that nearly led to the destruction of this community's most precious resource, Mr. Lester, and I *ain't talking trees, sir!*"

"...out of town...not having the courage to account... actions...unforgivable..."

Lester's response was garbled, but it was all moot anyway. Chute set forth a hard reality.

260 | ROBERT ESPENSCHEID JR.

"...liability...fight the charges. You have financial assets. You may have concluded that...lawful documentation to win a court case...with the storm, defense lawyers can scream 'Act of God' all they want, but mark my words, sir, when that jury gets a look at the scared faces and amputated limbs of fourteen-year-old Girl Scouts, you won't stand a *chance in hell of coming out of that courtroom alive!*"

Lester started, "We had the legal right..."

"Shut up, Dick. Your honor, Morgan Ivers from the parent company in Chicago. Let's cut to the quick. Your suggestions to resolve, sir."

"You have lives to repair and a town to recommit to, Mr. Ivers. I don't want these kids and their families to even see a medical bill. That gal Autumn Hook will surely require counseling in carrying on with her life. I expect Heartland to assist her in every..."

We moved off. Wasn't our place to act like peeping toms. Besides, we'd heard enough. Zeb had a half smile, gratified that the judge was cracking the whip where it belonged. Our club prez was not violent by nature, but with offspring in peril, he'd turn. Heartland's head was history. Chute was making sure of that. The sooner the better. Zeb crossing paths with Lester might prove explosive. He'd more than likely take a swing at him if given the chance.

That left me. Walking back out into the sunshine, I said, "Before you spread me on the rack, at least let me apologize."

"I want you to know, Hamilton, my mind wandered at times during the hearing, conjuring up ways to do you in. I concluded that six feet under was too shallow. Go twelve, I thought. Bury him double-deep. You knew the Scout troop was behind this. You never let on. *My own kid.* You want to apologize? Take the warrior way out, Straydog. Fall on your sword."

"I don't own a sword."

"Get one."

I grimaced. "Yes, at least that would be respectable."

Zeb stopped walking and grabbed my arm. We were face to face. "Maybe I'll bide my time until Miss Spinnetti finally caves and submits to your prodigious charms. The two of you conceive a daughter. I wait fourteen years; then stash her underneath a falling redwood."

He wasn't joking. "I see. The ol' eye for an eye. Jesus, Zeb, never in my wildest..."

"Stuff it, Hamilton. What do you make of those two?" He pointed over to where Harlin Shifter and Robin Emerson stood in animated discourse.

I gladly welcomed the switch in subject matter. "Well, they're a match to be sure, but it might take them an eternity to discover the obvious."

Zeb nodded. "Hope not."

"They're SMOs," I offered. "Soul mates with obstacles. That's one for Ana. Let her know."

262 | ROBERT ESPENSCHEID JR.

"She'll no doubt put it to use. Teens. My techie daughter texts me an instant message. Takes me an hour to decipher it."

We continued on to the parking lot. Zeb said, "I'll probably go the democratic route. Let the Dry Dogs decide your fate."

"What's the consensus?"

"All I know is that Shifter is set to resurrect Aaron Burr, dueling pistols cocked and primed."

"Ouch. Not surprised. I've lots of fence to mend."

"I reckon."

There was his half-smile again. "You're shameless, Story."

SUMMER '01

25
THE JACKASS ALLIANCE

I wish I was able to relay that the summer of 01 was all satisfied smiles and victory hugs. On the positive side, though storm-torn with broken branches hanging aloft at odd angles as if raked by some giant claw, the old oaks still stood. Given time and nature's way, they'll replenish greenery and repair themselves. But truth be told, though May had ended and sweet June blossomed in earnest, bad tidings engulfed the Jackass Alliance.

Lily had a second bout of pneumonia that frightened everyone to the core. Both Gordon and Autumn slipped into a blue funk, and snarled, "bug-off!" to anyone who entered their space.

Romance slithered away. Zeb and Jessi drifted. Robin, home alone with the kids and despairing a broken marriage, choose to stay planets apart from everyone, especially Harlin Shifter. My sun, Juliet, was lost to her study group while preparing for the bar exam. Even Madison and Riley remained clueless wonders. I felt the last bus had left Sugar City with *Love* on-board, waving goodbye. Heartbreaking.

The summer solstice had come and gone and somehow, that massive, dark thundercloud still hovered over all our heads.

Worrywart Weber ran amok all early summer acting like everyone's guardian angel, trying to atone for her self-perceived monumental screw-up at Wildnut. At some point, the great buttinski, making little headway and worn down by remorse, spun 180 degrees and vanished. Perhaps all it took was the piercing look of disapproval from a passerby on a Sugar City sidewalk. The small-town dark side, the small-town everyone-knows-and-has-an-opinion-and-there-is-no-place-to-hide dark side.

For those seriously hurt, all of us aped Madison and overplayed the nursemaid card. Annoyed to the max, Autumn and Gordon collaborated and sent everyone a postcard that screamed: GET OVER IT! GET A LIFE! ALL IS FINE!

But they really weren't.

In late June, doctors performed a third exploratory on Estey's back, grappling with more bone fragments. Confined to hospital bed and chair, he was like a giant catfish in shallow waters. Lily, when she was able to muster the energy, visited with a net full of books. Estey, with little choice, acquiesced. Walking was still a wishful dream, but slowly, the will to read grabbed a foothold.

Later, discharged and back home, depression got the best of him. In his eyes, he'd become nothing more than a poster-boy for the unread: "Oh, I know you; you're that nitwit that can't...," and all the variations on that theme. Gordon Estey took stock and stayed put. An attempt by town officials to recognize his heroism during the storm went unheeded. The one time Lily and I went knocking on his door, the big guy made it plain. He was alone and wanted to be left alone.

Pretty much all the Dry Dogs hunkered down with the blues. And why not, at the bottom of everything else, all the motorcycles lay piled in a mangled heap.

AUTUMN

Autumn too was a recluse. Small town or not, we'd seen little and heard less. Then, by happenstance, on a cool mid-July day, I stopped at Wildnut Park for another session of self-induced solitude and reflection. A few picnickers were there, also Ms. Hook, parked at a table alone. I approached. She was wearing faded jeans with a long sleeved yellow plaid flannel shirt topped with a brown leather vest. One scruffy Red Wing patted the ground, just one. We sat together. A pair of worn crutches stood propped up against a tree. Hard to fathom this serene spot held such terror for the two of us only a short time ago.

She told me she was being fitted for a prosthetic, that it hurt, that she hated the ugly thing, that the rehab physical therapy was excruciating, and that the doctors could take their phantom-pain explanations and shove it. I was aware that school softball was in full swing, that basketball practice was right around the corner and that one super talented tall blond presence would be missing both—for forever. I got a lump in my throat the size of a giant gum ball. "I'm at a loss, Autumn, at finding words to help..."

"Guess what one of the nurses called it? Hah. An appliance. Can you imagine?" She tossed her head back. "I'm half girl, half *appliance*, Mr. Hamilton."

I had no answer for that one.

She appeared to sag in self-defeat. "Look, do one thing for me, Mr. Hamilton."

"Can we loosen the reins here? Call me Alex, Straydog, anything."

"Sure. Your name is so cool. It's all the *on's*, don't ya think? Washingt*on*, Jeffers*on*, you."

"Imagine, Hook, the country's very independence...resting on my wobbly shoulders."

"I dub thee Founding Father Alex."

"Right. You were asking: one thing?"

"Yeah. Stop blaming yourself. Tough enough dealing with Maddy's guilt trip. Nobody's at fault, 'cept maybe that Heartland guy who started the whole mess."

"Damn, that's the one thing I can't provide, Autumn. For me right now, guilt is good. Guilt keeps me beholden to you, and the truth is, I like the feeling; I need that feeling. Guilt's like a lifeline to see this through." I sighed. "Make any sense?"

I got a quizzical stare and a, "Not really." Moments passed in silence between us, then she offered, "So you're up for most anything, huh? For sure?"

"Absolutely. Name it."

"On my eighteenth birthday, I want you to buy me a new Ford Mustang: dark green, light-brown leather seats, stick-shift, maxed-out CD sound system, *and*...this is vital...a convertible. Got to be a convertible. I want all the bells and whistles, Father Alex. Don't go thrifty on me."

I laughed and shook my head. "You are good, Hook. Really good. Check with me when the day arrives. I might be able to spring for the air in the tires."

Her expression reverted to consternation. She asked, "Maybe you can help me out with something else?"

"I'm all ears."

"The male species."

"Uh-oh."

"Know what's kinda buggin' me? I'm like, almost fourteen and I'm growing up, you know, blooming; and every time I'm in a group with guys, all they show an interest in is my stump."

I knew she was dead serious. "Never underestimate the loutish behavior of the typical American young buck, Miss Hook. Course, you're part Terminator now. If they become a problem, put the fear of Arnold in them."

"I'm an amp. A freak!"

Her intensity startled me. Oh how I wanted to say the right words and give her comfort, but I truly felt like a man stranded in a land that spoke a foreign language. This was so hard. "Look, when everything turns to shit, just stare in the mirror and say: Alexander Hamilton thinks I'm awesome."

"Yeah, right. Besides, you already got an awesome girl. Maddy told me."

"Please, Hook, forget my romantic melodrama. I'm really trying here, okay?"

"Gotcha."

With the afternoon waning, taking with it the midday breeze, the oak trees stood patiently still as if to listen in as I fumbled for words. "My guess is you will turn eighty and still regret your loss. The hurt will never go away. And another guess is that along the way, there will be plenty of guys who won't give you a second look cause you're damaged goods. And a third guess says that you will accept this with a lot of anger and tears. But listen close, Miss Hook, also traveling down the highway will come a few dudes from out of nowhere, who won't give an owl's hoot about five missing toes cause their too charmed, too mesmerized, and too freaking out-of-control in *love* with rubbing and kissing the five ya got!"

Catching my breath our eyes met and I got a contemplative look from her. She hugged herself, bending at the waist, and stared at her boot for a spell—then tilted her head back my way and said, "Are they going to show up before or after I get the Mustang?"

Oh man, our tears flowed from laughter, and right then I felt an awareness I hadn't had for weeks and weeks. Hope? Maybe. I was thrilled at our having met up. For sure, she was set to scratch the world's eyes out, but she had managed, in her own way, to convey that all was not lost, that her spirit was intact. I rebuked her earlier assertion with all the persuasiveness I could muster. "You're not a freak, Autumn Hook. You are rock solid okay."

WILDNUT(S)

Dick Lester was recalled to Chicago. No one in Sugar City paid his future much mind. Paul Weber, Madison's dad, was named interim manager. Paul's first order of business was to authorize the construction of a bridge over the Horn River.

During the last week of July, with foundation work well underway, the company began a supplies inventory. One such mission to a nearly forgotten storeroom led to a startling discovery.

"Jesus, what's that?!"

"Find a poker. I think it's dead."

"No, no. Check it out. It's sleeping."

"Let me see. Well, I'll be damned."

"What?"

"Who's got a cell? Call that Willie Ribbs fellah over at the manor place."

Turns out the stock room guys had been providing food and water to a stray cat they'd named Wire. But all this time, Wire never let on he was sharing. Leave it to Slacker Red to locate the vittles.

He'd been boarding there for weeks, roaming the Heartland plant at night. Finding treasures. Some of the gals in the office were missing these stuffed-animal Beanie Babies from their desks. They'd begun good-naturedly teasing one another over pilfering. Red had them all piled up together where he slept.

MIRACULOUS DISCOVERY was a front page banner under the fold in our weekly Sugar City Sun. The weasel reacted to all the attention and affection with a mighty yawn. Didn't matter. Red was back home. The world was a better place.

So Dick Lester got lost and Red was found. For Sugar City—not a bad exchange, and if locating the slacker meant a lot to a few folk, what was taking shape out at Wildnut Park gave everyone in our small burg pause to wonder.

Across Iowa, Judge Chute's inquiry became a cause célèbre as the media revisited the park storm with stories about *The Tree That Refused to Fall,* and *Defenders from the Fury: Old Oaks Safeguard Troop 822.* Far as I know, no one has yet written about the tree branches that saved our biker butts. Guess that's our lot in life. We can live with it.

Considering the publicity KBOX generated, recounts were natural, but remarkably, folks began arriving at Wildnut to check out where all the drama had taken place. State climatologists have calculated the May 11 wind shear as the strongest on historical record. Some cars stopping by even sported out-of-state plates.

Lonnie Shimmer chain-sawed the fallen sentinel into thousands of pieces, occasionally refilling a wooden bucket so visitors might take home a souvenir. Iowa's a peculiar place, tourist-wise. We have no Grand Canyon, no Devil's Tower, no Empire State Building, no Golden Gate Bridge. There's nothing really to gawk at. But oddly, amongst the barns and beans, tourists drive from all over to share a few moments with a covered bridge and/or a ball diamond. They're both long stories, and I'm not going to bend your ear. Suffice it to say, imagined by way of books and movies, an old bridge in Winterset and a ballpark in Dyersville have come to represent something meaningful to people; an emotional tie to loves lost and found.

Maybe our park is becoming another symbol, one of natural heritage and the importance of hanging onto it. People arrive with picnic baskets. They stand at the very spot I stood on that fateful day. One can look up to the gaping hole in the canopy created by the tree tumbling down from the sky. The viewer can spot any number of broken limbs still wedged in the arms of its brethren. So most folks grab a twig for inspiration or as a reminder perhaps. Either one's good.

As for me, I will revisit each future May 11 to acknowledge the trees for making that desperate grab as the sentinel came ripping through, eternally thankful that they *held*. Many scoff at such a notion. Logic wills that it was all happenstance. Oh, ye of little faith. Explain Gordon's miracle push-up? How about that tangy apple! Stubborn realists bestow the laurels to the potency of adrenalin. That's laughable. The answer is simple: If the trees can *hold*, they can also *lift*.

Gordon Estey's self-imposed exile was a constant worry. Lilly's phone calls went unanswered. Scheduled rehabs were missed. Shifter, infuriated at the self-pitying lard, actually blasted into Estey's digs cradling a chainsaw and cleaved his television in half (thank God he first pulled the plug), threatening Dimmer with the same fate if he didn't get his dead ass in gear.

But nothing worked. As Will Ribbs explained: "I knew Harlin had been attempting everything under the sun to get Estey turned. Others, too. No progress. The guy's a tough nut. Well, so is depression. I've come across this mind-set many times with young vets and old folk. Gordon is a proud dude. He'd spent his whole life using brawn. Now, flat on his back, that power was gone. He worried me. Emotions can play havoc. There develops this overwhelming fear of the future. Last thing we needed was a shadowy suicide-watch, but assuming time alone might help was chancy."

Though I'm eons removed from Gordon's burden, there are times I share his despair. I've grown weary with court-ordered community service while barely managing to keep my small engine repair shop afloat. Riley Blue's been a godsend helping out this summer. But the culprit of my melancholy rests with the heart. Both Juliet and her pal Sticker passed the Bar. No surprise there. Jules called, full of excitement. She will soon be off righting injustice, I'm sure. Dare to be great, Miss Spinnetti. It's all happening, and I feel the chill of loneliness and separation growing colder.

Laboring away, shoring up heartbreak, I've taken to pondering my own future. Returning to school was near the top of my doables. But the more I thought of stuffy classrooms and expensive ivy-covered walls, the less appealing academia looked. Truth is, I don't want to leave Sugar City right now.

Too many unfinished stories are playing out. Too many lives appear wobbling on the high wire. Besides, for me, Slacker Red's return was an omen. A wink of good fortune had managed to slither past the omnipotent dark cloud controlling our lives. Moreover, that sliver of blue sky overhead began to widen.

Case in point: In a surprise mid-August turnabout, word got out. Jessi and Zeb were married. Zeb had fulfilled a longtime father-to-daughter promise as he and Ana journeyed to Santa Ana, Mexico. Ana had been named for this village where her mom was born and came of age. Jessi and Rachel traveled with them. On the return, having pre-planned it all, they tied the knot out at Bonita Lake near Ruidoso, New Mexico. They had told no one their plans and totally electrified the kids. Jessi told me later, with a satisfied grin, how she and Zeb had played and won the ultimate game of "Gotcha" on their two would-be matchmakers: "We arrived at Ruidoso with both girls still clueless and whining, 'Why are we stopping here? We need to get home.' Then Zeb throws on his gray tux jacket formal that he'd hidden away, and I began waving a bridal veil in their faces. What a hoot. Needless to say, teenage OMG's ruled the day. The girls flipped a coin, Alex. Ana was Best Man and my wonderful Rachel gave away her dear ol' mom."

So there you have it. I was blissfully mistaken. Love hadn't been bused out of town. Love was still around playing hide-and-seek: *Close your eyes, kids. Count to one hundred. Here I come.*

During August too, Robin Emerson and Harlin Shifter were an item and tongues were wagging as only tongues can in small-town Iowa. I'm not going to speculate as to their future together. I know on occasion they roll out the patched up Harleys, drop the kids at grandmama's, and go riding.

Robin Monnington Emerson's world has flipped upside-down. Her family had been shaken by Wayne's leaving, then was left confused and perplexed over this biker creature. But it's well to remember a couple facts: One, the Monningtons are a large fourth-generation Century Farm family; and two, Harlin Shifter puts food on the table as a professional welder. In short, a bunch of neglected projects are getting glued back together down at the Monnington Spread. Robin's suitor is gaining stature by the day. Olin Spoon saw him the other day down at the Dairy Cup with Robin's kids; hair slicked back, driving a Dodge Caravan.

Oh yeah. With the game on the line, on a three-and-two count, Cupid has no fear of throwing the change-up curve.

THE LIBRARIAN

And if Gordon Dimmer Estey felt secure in his rabbit hole, he was sadly mistaken. Without warning a cyclone named Dixanne Bracket blew into his life. At first, as with the rest of us, she was stonewalled. He dismissed her overtures. Whoever she was, whatever she wanted, the phone calls all pointed to more Jackass harassment.

How did Dixie, our Sugar City librarian, transform the conflicted recluse into a larger-than-large Dr. Seuss?

She explained: The lummox. Never returning my calls. I was running out of time and needed to get one-on-one with him. But how? In the end the answer proved so simple. It was on my computer screen staring at me all summer. He had an overdue book. Something checked out years ago. So I left a message. Said he owed $3000 in back fines, that the library needed an endowment for a new wing, and I was coming over to collect, that this would be his last chance for a settlement before I turned the matter over to the Capone Collection Agency. God bless his gullible heart; he believed my every word.

I was running a summer reading program for fourth, fifth, and sixth graders who needed a boost. My efforts were going nowhere fast. Gordon Estey was the answer to prodding my remedial Storyfest off the starting blocks. I told him so. He looked at me like I was loco.

"Me?!"

"Yes, you."

"You know who you're talking to, Ms. Brackett?"

"Mr. Gordon Estey, I presume."

"But I've never taught anything, much less kids, much less reading. Have you been out of town all year? This is a joke, right?"

"This is no joke, young man. Who better to reach struggling youngsters than someone who's worn their very shoes? I know you've a tutor. Time to put that learnin' to good use, Mr. Estey."

Gordon's face crumbled. "I can't. I could never do what you're asking. Please. Forget it. My messing up at Wildnut was bad enough."

"Now you just listen to me. As a child in grade school, perhaps even middle school, you had an attention disorder. That's not uncommon, and they come in all shapes and sizes. And, Mr. Estey, like a pair of old trousers, you simply grew out of it. The maze that haunted you has vanished. Lily tells me you're gaining reading skills by leaps and bounds. Now's the time to shine, bucko. Give these kids a swat and a boost. A push you never had. It'll be good for you. Great for them."

"But..."

"No buts."

I didn't want to resort to my bottom line but this man-child was obviously the symbol I'd been keeping watch for. I'd laid bare my odd premonitions to my compatriots at the last county librarian get-together. The girls were near set to pack me off to Bellevue. Hah! Now, my foreseen flag-bearer had arrived and I *had* to reach him.

"You want these kids to wind up like you...to go through what you've been through all these years?"

"Of course not. HEY! That's not fair, Ms. Brackett."

"Call me Dixie. We're going to make a great team, Gordon Estey."

And sure enough, they did.

Not at first, though. Not hardly. Starting out, the kids didn't know what to make of their hulking mentor. The novelty soon wore off, because here was a guy who struggled at reading just as poorly as themselves. Elementary-aged moppets have lots of places to be in the summer. The library, on a made-to-order-outdoor-pool-day, is not one of them. Gordon Estey had taken on a tough task. The sessions were fizzling out. The program had no spark.

No spark until an August day when Madison Weber made a brief, rare public appearance and presented Gordon and his class with a CD: The Donnas, *Get Skintight*. "You can read anything," Maddy said. "Try working your way through the lyrics. This is cool fun stuff."

That's what they did.

That was the spark.

They'd sit around a conference table at the library, listen to a song, then read the lyrics out loud. Regardless of the reader, when a mess up occurred, the cry (aping the band), "You're a zero on my rock-o-meter" rang loud and clear. Dixie said she wasn't sure what was going on, but there sure was a lot of laughter leaking through the walls.

Madison's offering up the Donnas proved to be the tip of the iceberg. Gordon had noticed the library stocked books-on-tape. Folks were checking them out for long car trips. The recordings hatched an idea: locate a few microphones and a recorder, then have the kids each take a reading role to narrate a story.

So, they took a shot. They began easy with a Seuss, then began prowling the bookshelves for others. Maybe it was the mistake-prone stuttering early playbacks, or the fact that as the kids listened they sensed themselves gaining somehow. Whatever. The audio storytelling clicked from the start. Everyone read parts. The kids dived in with relish. They worked like bees.

Funny how life works out sometimes. How weaknesses can turn to strengths. How when we least expect it, talents emerge we never knew existed.

MADDY

A week prior to Labor Day, Madison Weber stopped by the shop hoping to find Riley. She was nonchalant over showing up, as if her two-month-absence was of little import. Man, talk about a sight for sore eyes. There was just the two of us. Riley was off on a resupply mission over at Paterno's Hardware.

"Let him know I was here, Mr. Hamilton. Will ya?"

Rattled over her showing up, I found myself questioning, after all this time, if she were flesh and blood or an apparition. I wanted to reach out, grab her shoulders and shake her—somehow shock myself into believing the girl was real. She was halfway out the door before I managed to gasp, *"Wait!* Not another step. You expect me to tell Blue you were here and that I let you go? He'll quit and never work for me again."

She was no ghost. Madison wore brown overalls over a white tee, black high-top sneaks, no hat. The buzz punk hair, so stylish at the hearing, had begun to shag out. She acted distant and worn out. But her facial scars had taken a hike, and if there was a more fetching fourteen-year-old lass amongst the tall prairie grass, I don't know where she'd be. She appeared to be in a quandary for a few moments, then wandered over and sat to wait by the workbench. I hollered at her, "I'm gonna raid the fridge. Want a beer?" No answer. The icy air escaping the mini felt refreshing. I was poking around the canned inventory. "Is it too carly?"

"I don't drink beer, and you'd better watch it, Mr. Hamilton. I told my mom you were building me a chopper. She believes you're a corrupting influence."

"Praise be. I knew there was a reason I was on this mortal coil. Diet Pepsi? All we got. It's cold."

"Sold."

"Good. There's two. Think I'll join you." I grabbed a battered metal fold-up, slid it across from her, and parked my butt. For a bit we sipped in silence.

Judge Chute had cast us the architects of the ill-fated struggle to save Wildnut Park, and maybe because of that, we had shied away from one another all summer; as if personal contact might further fester our already guilt-ridden psyches.

No "How ya doin'," no "Long time no see," Madison chimed right in. "I'm banned from Lily's house probably forever. I told her mom and dad I would never endanger anyone, especially Lily; that Lily is my best friend and I miss her." She turned to the shop windows facing Main Street with a faraway gaze. "Lily's mom said I was reckless, that..." She wasn't even looking at me, just going on and on as if this was all she had thought about for weeks and now it all came gushing out. "...that Lily would follow me over a cliff, and, as a mom, that scared her. She said I didn't treat Lily's trust with the respect that it deserves, and here's the cruncher, Mr. Hamilton: 'Using Lily to further your own agenda is not friendship, Madison.'" She spun at me teary eyed and resigned. "And you know what, Mr. Hamilton? She's right. She's right about everything."

Took me half a minute to absorb the tantrum. "Ah horseshit, and drop the mister, will you please? What is it with you girls? Look, Weber, the storm hit one hundred days ago, but Lily's mom is still frightened. Maybe we all are. Don't fret. Nothing in the long run is going to keep you and Miss Starr apart. I remember May 11 like it was yesterday. You cradling her, comforting her, quietly talking, imagining... no...*willing* a future. I was right there with you when Will plunged that shiv."

Madison visibly paled.

"You'll both work this out with parents and stuff. Count on it."

"What if she'd *died*?! And Autumn!"

I sat back. Her fury was shocking. A shouting match was entirely unexpected but here we were. "She *lived*! They all survived. *Hey!* If you've the weight-of-the-world on your shoulders, join the club, Weber. You and I should start a band: The Guilt Trippers."

The girl turned away. "Can we change the subject?"

The raw anguish inside her seemed to deflate as fast as it had come on. "Let's."

"Thank you. The Jackass Alliance is pairing off. You and Jules better get with the program."

"Now I'm calling for a subject change."

"Uh-uh. No way."

I detected a whiff of a smile from her. I sighed, "My Drake Law squeeze is in deliberation. It takes two, Madison."

"She'll come around."

I gave her my best eagle-eye. "How so?"

All I got back from teen loveline was a shoulder shrug and, "Girl talk."

We drank our cola and let the warm afternoon steal away. I finally said, "I want you to know I'm proud of you." She cocked her head, confused. "Proud of everything you've done, everything you're doing."

"Subject change."

"No, Weber. I mean what I say. I know you're harboring lots of blame. Me too. But Lily's mom is wrong. You're not reckless. You are a risk taker. You are not afraid to do what you believe is right, and if the venture fails, well, you're there to pick up the pieces. That's a couple of pretty good virtues, kiddo. Plus rescuing Gordon and the kids over at the library...yeah, I heard...with the rock lyric thing. That's not happening from someone set to toss in the towel...a giver-upper."

I was hoping for a rise out of her, but she remained mum. Aggravating. "Hey! Where's this Voice of Reason I keep hearing about?"

Nothing. Madison the Sphinx.

"Okay, you, maybe I'm on the wrong highway here. Tell you what. I take it all back. Next time I start my day agonizing over Estey and Hook, I'll remind myself: *You're not the lowest of the low, Hamilton. Weber's hurting worse than you.* Hah! This idea ain't bad. Think about it. No matter how down I get, I've always got you to fall back on."

"I can do the same."

Bingo. "Damn straight. The Guilt Trippers. Our own exclusive depression cult. We'll rise on a ladder from our abyss by striving to keep one rung-up on each other."

"You're at the bottom, Hamilton."

"How so, Weber?"

Mocking me, the kid got her two-cents in. "I'm not laboring guilt *and* tarring roofs in a summer heat wave."

I grinned. "You're right. I am the bottom-griever."

That produced a good-natured laugh from both of us. I took advantage. "I want to say a couple things about the storm before Riley returns. That okay?"

"Maybe."

"Great. Here goes. First off I believe, no ifs, ands, or buts, that the trees protected us that terrible day. All our lives were saved by the slimmest of margins. And two, that the oak grove didn't make that effort just so those of us still standing might run away and hide in sorrow and remorse."

And with that, the two of us, perhaps forever linked, finally began speaking from our hearts. We talked of old timber, of fate and second chances, of obligations and accountability, of judgments and of being judged. I believe I put aside the Men-

Are–from-Mars persona and shed a few tears. Madison, too. We posed more questions to each other than answers. Recalling how the old sentinel was stayed from causing irrevocable harm; in life, I guess, sometimes the only explanation for certain events is—that there is none. Then Madison tossed more seasoning in the soup. "I don't want to grow up feeling I need to discover a cure for cancer."

We hardly needed this. "Don't go Freudian on me, Weber. Right now we focus day-to-day on Lily, Autumn, and Gordon. The storm was a random act. Isolated 120 mph wind shears have no premeditation. We all fell. Now we're in the process of standing back up. Don't you dare allow that day, that dark cloud, to dominate and set the course of your life. Besides, if anyone in the Jackass Alliance is going to cure cancer, it'll be...," I held out the palm of my hands:

"Lily Starr!" We both shouted her name at once, looked at one another, and smiled.

"Doubled up on the carb cleaner, Alex. Got a deal and... hey, Madison. What's going on, guys?"

Absorbed, we hadn't heard Riley return.

"Life, Blue. Toss it all on the bench and take the rest of the day. You and Madison run on. Enjoy yourselves."

"You sure?"

"Yep. I'm locking up early."

"Cool."

They were halfway out the door when I shouted, "Hold on, before you both split. Subject change, Weber: Emma Cogswell."

"Who?"

"Turned one hundred years of age last week. Still spry. Cogswells celebrated with a family reunion picnic at Wildnut Park. Big family. Lots of friends. Heard tell some seventy five folks partook the burgers and potato salad. They all had plenty of shade. Shade is good. Remember that, Miss Weber."

She caught my eye. "Words to live by, Mr. Hamilton?"

"We could do worse, Miss Weber."

Let's sing a song of long ago
When trees could grow
And days flowed quietly

Randy Newman
Dayton, Ohio—1903

26
THE RIDE

Beginning the second full week in September, on a warm
Sunday afternoon, Scout Troop 822 and the Dry Dog Blues
motorcycle club gathered once again at Wildnut Park. As
a token of solidarity, Lonnie Shimmer and a couple of his
loggers had dug a deep hole to help plant a new tree. We'd
all chipped in and bought a healthy looking fifteen-footer to
replace the lost sentinel. The young oak sapling was set to rise
one hundred feet and stand tall for one hundred years.

Autumn's grandpa taxied all the Scouts in the old farm
flatbed, the same truck heisted by the gals that not so long
ago May day. Everyone was there, including wheelchair-bound
Gordon. We noted he'd brought along a walker. Rumors had
spread he was progressing. Was the walker proof positive he
was able to stand? Take a step? The Jackass Alliance wanted to
know.

Estey balked at first. We were allowing none of that and
gathered around him, chanting, "Show us! Show us! Show us!"

"All right. All right. Back off. Gimme some space, dag
nabbit. Bunch of hooligans."

Watching him grab the walker with one hand and hang onto Harlin Shifter with the other, then rise, was a religious experience. He steadied, found his bearing, and took a few tentative steps. Harlin let go. Gordon repositioned and straight-armed the walker. He was off.

Almost like he'd planned, he tracked slowly to Rachel and Lily. Reaching them he leaned forward, slightly bowed, acknowledging them with a soft head-butt and a high-five. He then made his way toward Autumn. "You and me, Miss Hook. A foot race. Thirty yards. Thanksgiving Day. We'll square off at your place, out at the farm. Run off all that turkey and mashed potatoes. What-a-ya-say? The simp takes on the gimp. Winner gets first in line for apple pie."

Autumn dissolved in tears. "You are *so on*, Mr. Estey."

He managed a 180-degree turnabout, and huffing and puffing, fought gamely back to his chair.

Damn, it was hard not to leap up and cheer.

Lily, though wafer-thin, looked radiant. Juliet rode down from Drake. We'd invited Judge Chute to the dedication. He thanked us graciously but declined, saying he would be an intrusion; that the Alliance alone ought to partake in the rebirth. He asked to be remembered, wished everyone well, and inquired if we'd mind his checking in on us from time to time. Zeb, who'd made the call, replied that as long as he wasn't handing down indictments, any overture on his part was welcome.

Madison wanted Riley to attend but he declined for the same reasons. Only this time we didn't take no for an answer.

Jessi thought it'd be great to get a group picture and Riley finally agreed to tag along as chief photog.

In the late afternoon, trees gently swaying from a pleasant breeze, we stood right where the storm had ripped up the old oak that nearly sent us all to our maker. I immediately thought the hole dug was too deep and said so, but Autumn, bearing up with a newly-fitted, carbon-fiber limb, scolded, "No, it's perfect." She had hauled in an ice-cooler. With a mischievous gleam in her eye and a maniacal grin, she reached down into the cubes, shouting , *"Aha!!"* She stood and raised up high a large, clear plastic bag filled with fluid and her severed leg.

If she hoped for a stunned reaction, she sure as hell got one.

Ribbs chose a medical close-up. Troop 822 slowly back peddled the opposite direction "God, Auti," "Totally gross," "Retch city," then commenced a full out revolted, hasty retreat.

Autumn loved the shock; chasing after the cowards with a robotic Igor strut, laughing insanely, sloshing her lost lower limb about with ghoulish glee.

Who knows? Perhaps we were witnessing grief-related progress. Demented to be sure, but progress nonetheless. In retrospect, Autumn's surprise and plan were both pure of heart. Embracing one's grief. That's probably a good thing. Surely one's better running amok, terrifying friends, than plastering on a brave face while silently screaming on the inside. Burying her loss deep beneath the young sapling made righteous sense.

Later, maybe 'cause I was somehow the natural choice, I was set to offer a dedication. As I surveyed this group, I knew right then that whatever future plans lay in store for me, they had to begin in Sugar. Here was my anchor.

I'd hardly begun when Madison interrupted. "Ah, Father Alex, before this tree blessing thing gets underway, Auti and I have a couple of bits. Okay?"

"Roger that, Weber. The stage is yours."

Madison looked to her compatriot. "We're still gonna do this. Right, Hook?"

"Are you?"

"Yeah. I guess."

"Here we go, then. Gramps. Go get it."

Errol Hook gave a happy wink, quick-stepped to the flatbed cab, and returned with a chair and a cello. We fanned out in anticipation as Autumn positioned herself saying only, "I'm just starting out. Don't expect a whole lot." She took a deep breath, closed her eyes, and began playing.

Our gathering, the light of day, the stillness, the music, all interwove into one of those magic moments you just wrap yourself around. Autumn concluded, embarrassed by our bravos, and if our applause was somewhat hushed, it probably stemmed from our pastoral setting and the fact that the girl had cast a reverent spell with her playing.

She remained seated with bow in hand as Madison then stood up next to her and said, "For all you tin-eared metalheads out there, we just heard *The Swan*, from the *Carnival of Animals Symphony* in G-major by Camille Saint-Saens. The indomitable Miss Autumn Hook on the cello."

Standing before us, Madison, obviously nervous, pulled out a crumbled yellow-lined sheet of paper from her back pocket. Whatever she was going to say, she had it written down. No improvising here. This was important. The two girls had planned this performance. Madison had nailed the French composer's name. That took practice. Holding her written speech by her side, she fidgeted about as if she were having second thoughts about saying anything. Finally. "Okay guys, first off, I'm not going to rehash anymore I'm-sorry-stuff."

Rachel shouted, "You *better* can that wimpy whine, Webslinger."

Madison nodded and forged ahead. "I bumped into my high school English teacher this summer. Ms. Rhubottom. She acted all girly. 'Oh Madison, I'm looking forward to a wonderful year. So glad to have you in class. I'm hoping you'll provide an essay about that dreadful experience in Wildnut Park'—blah blah blah. At first I thought, *This is high school.* She can't be proposing one of those goofy 'How I Spent My Summer Vacation' bores. But, holy Barbie, she did, and now I'm on the hook. But what happened was...Ms. Rhubottom got me thinking about May 11 and something popped up I'd totally forgot about. As the tree was falling, Rachel's mom screamed, "Run!" Ana and I grabbed hands and we lit out. Right then, over the winds roar, I heard someone call out, 'My saddlebags. Grab them. Save the beer.'" She paused (rather dramatically). "Anyone want to own up? Was that you, Lily?"

Conjuring up her best southern drawl, Lily purred, "No, Miss Weber. 'Twasn't me. Gracious. I don't recall bringing any beer to the park."

The leather clad Dry Dogs all looked like their hand was caught in the proverbial cookie jar. Some were gazing at cloud formations. Others were shifting dirt with their boots. A little whistling was detected.

Madison almost smiled. "Anyway, here's what I'm going to lay on Rhubottom's writing class." She unfolded her hand-held notes, collected herself, and began reading:

If it had to be somebody, I'm glad it was us. What if the monster wind had ripped the roof off the elementary school and killed a bunch of those kids? But it saw us instead. We were the very young striving to save the very old. The storm thought it had found an easy mark. It was wrong. A great tragedy overtook us unexpectedly. But the evil force that bred terror was met head-on by those who kept cool and reacted with honor and grace. I am privileged to be part of such a group.

She concluded, slowing herself down, measuring each word.

So, if you're caught out in the open, facing down
the biggest, baddest thunderstorm ever to hit
Iowa, make sure you surround yourself with—
Friends who are super brave
Friends whose hearts are bigger than the Scout
vests they wear
Friends whose hearts are stronger than the
machines they ride
Friends who are too busy helping to show fear
And lastly, no matter the trial
Friends who are rockin' enough to save the damn
beer.

She looked up. "That's it. All yours, Father Alex."

Jessi acted for us all as she reached for Madison and gave her a smothering hug. Buried in Jessi's arms, our eyes met, and I hope my expression conveyed that she had given the best speech ever.

"Couple of tough acts to follow, eh, Hamilton?"

"My lot in life, Story. Alright folks, grab a tool. Here we go."

I bent down, scooping soil into a paper cup. Raising Mother Earth high above my head, I said, "To history, heritage, harmony, and shade."

"Here-here's" and "Amens" rang out. I tossed the cup into the hole. With one last forlorn look, Autumn pitched in her leg. Shoveling commenced.

296 | ROBERT ESPENSCHEID JR.

Later, Riley positioned the Alliance together around the young freshly planted oak for the photo shoot. At the last second Ana shouted, "Wait, we forgot Red." Sacked out in his pickup, Will ran to fetch him. A *Me-me-me!* soon had the slacker snuggled in Ana's arms. We were now complete and Blue's shot proved a good one: a few smiles, a few weary proud looks, a few lost in contemplative thought. I'm sure we'll all keep our prints in a treasured spot.

With our dedication complete, we were set to drift apart when Juliet Spinnetti reminded me of our agreement back in early May—and that she was ready to collect.

I didn't know what she was talking about until she pointed out that I owed her a solo ride on my Harley in exchange for the legal expertise she'd provided. "Remember, Alexander Hamilton? Iowa law? Kidnapping?"

Yikes! That phone call request seemed like a million years ago. I stammered that maybe this wasn't the best time or place, but the Blue's and Scouts all sided with Jules and were having none of my reneging. "Pay up, Hamilton," was the consensus.

She grabbed Robin's helmet and straddled the Soft Tail. I carefully pointed out the controls and solemnly reminded her as to all the repair work recently completed; that my precious machine had had the misfortune of being crushed under a fallen oak tree and now, up and running once again, had zero craving for toppling over in a heap.

The Jackass Alliance showed no sympathy for my pleas.

Spinnetti shouted, "Back off, Straydog. I'm heading out." She hit the start button. The Harley rumbled to life like J. J.

Cale. She thunkered down into first, twisted a bit of gas, and slowly let go the clutch. From behind, I gave a gentle push as everything I dearly loved slowly took flight.

The Alliance cheered her on. I stood with fingers crossed, following her as she rolled north along the old factory road that wound up the hillside and out onto the highway. She reached third or fourth before downshifting and turned right onto Heartland's new entrance drive. We all sensed her gaining confidence, really moving now, the Harley barking out a steady cadence as she rounded a bend and swooped up onto the new bridge. Halfway across the beautiful dark red span, she let go her left hand, raised her fist high in the air, and howled out a mighty, *"Woooooooooooooooohaaaaaaaaaaaaaaaaaa!!"*

A moment—a sight—that for all of us—simply thrilled.

I know Juliet Spinnetti is not hanging out the legal shingle in Sugar City, at least not yet anyway. So, I'm preparing for the long haul. I know she has dreams. I know the Spinnetti clan back East wants her close to home. I know she's going. I just hope she leaves her heart in Iowa.

This is a work of fiction. All principle characters and events are products of the author's imagination with a few exceptions. Drake University exists, of course, situated comfortably within Des Moines, Iowa. Wanda Derry taught piano for years in Lamoni, and Murray High School is quite real and widely known for unleashing competitive basketball teams.

Robert Espenscheid lives in Lamoni, Iowa, traveling rural routes tuning and repairing (they're all worth saving) pianos. The *Jackass Alliance* is his first novel.

Visit him online at www.firejacker.net

Made in the USA
Charleston, SC
29 January 2015